SOUL OF A PRINCE

STEVE ROUBAI

Palmyra
Books

Palmyra Books
Canada
Copyright © 2010 Steve Roubai
steve_imex@hotmail.com
ISBN: 978-0-9867837-0-8
The Canadian ISBN Service System

Edited by Barb McLaren
mclarenba@hotmail.com

Original cover illustration by Jim Warren. Permission to use artwork for book cover granted by Jim Warren.
www.jimwarren.com

Printed in Canada

www.soulofaprince.com

SOUL OF A PRINCE

PROLOGUE

It was morning. A strange man walked into a café by the seashore, appearing to be looking for someone. Solomon was sitting, drinking a cup of tea. The strange man spotted Solomon and sat next to him. Solomon continued to sip his tea, never turning his head to acknowledge the man that sat next to him.

"Is it you?" asked the man.

Solomon pretended not to hear and continued to sip his tea.

"Are you the one?" asked the man.

Solomon again pretended not to hear, minding his own business.

"I know it's you," he said. "You're the soul reader. You communicate with the souls of the living."

Solomon placed his cup down onto the table and turned his head.

"What is the soul?" asked Solomon.

"I don't know," replied the man. I don't understand what it is.

"The soul is the nonphysical aspect of a human being," said Solomon. "It manifests as consciousness and the distinction between right and wrong. It is the human's emotional and moral essence, where the most private and personal thoughts and feelings are hidden and manifested.

Every human being recognizes the energy within. Some people learn to nurture it and accept its nature, and understand that a soul requires certain elements for its growth. A walk in the park or by the seashore, a loving friend to spend time with, a baby's smile, doing a charitable act or staring into a clear blue sunny sky, can all bring growth to the soul. When the mind, heart and body neglect the soul's need, the human suffers great distress. It is not materialistic. It is of the essence of the Higher Soul. The moments before sleep, a person evaluates life and the mistakes and successes they've made. It's at this point when the soul speaks to the person about the satisfaction or neglect it feels. We are on a journey. We are born into a world that teaches us to do what is right and forbid what is wrong, but most people do not learn. They're afraid of risk, fearing change, failure and loneliness. Simultaneously, they are unwilling to overcome their fear of change by accepting the inevitable, unwilling to overcome their fear of failure by accepting their human imperfections and unwilling to overcome their fear of loneliness by allowing new people to enter their lives. As a result, they risk the opportunity to travel to new places to see a sunrise from another part of the world, risk the opportunity to see the finer details in life and what makes it so incredible to live and risk the opportunity to fall in love or make a new friend. Every new experience nurtures the soul's growth. People need to listen more closely to their souls. I help them listen."

"Who are you?" asked the man in disbelief.

"I'm Solomon," he said.

CHAPTER 1 - THE BOY

Solomon was sitting by the window in his room staring out into the distance. It was a sunny clear day. The blue sky hovered above the land, and the clouds shape shifted across the field. A cooling wind passed by, blowing tree branches humbly to their sides.

In the distance, seagulls filled the sky, meandering. The green mountains in the distance surrounded the horizon. The fields were filled with olive trees. The smell of the wind was scented. The springs here were always delightful. Butterflies danced by. Birds chased after one another, branch to branch.

This was the Mediterranean, the most enchanting

place on earth. It was no wonder why so many people throughout history, had always been attracted to it, hot summers and warm winters.

The people of the Mediterranean had always been renowned for their beauty, with dark hair and big captivating eyes. They were also friendly people with incomparable hospitality. Families were close. Neighbors asked about one another and spent time on a daily basis discussing family, work, politics and even local gossip. The Mediterranean had always been renowned for gossip. People could spend hours each day discussing other people's lives and seemed to never tire or get bored.

Solomon was never fond of this. He found it a waste of time. However, that's how most people spent their time, by gossiping. Solomon was now fourteen years old. His birthday had just passed. He didn't celebrate it as most others would. His mother made him a cake.

Some people saw birthdays as a new year, a new beginning and a new opportunity. Other people viewed birthdays as another year closer to their deaths. Solomon was neither. He didn't see birthdays as a time to celebrate nor grieve. Rather, he saw every single day as a new chance to be happy or a new chance to change life around, at least that's what his mother always told him.

Whenever the sun rose, it brought light and warmth to the new day. Whenever the wind blew, it brought new hopes and new possibilities.

Nature was a wise creature. It taught man the very essence of life. Trees for instance, could live for hundreds of years, and quite possibly thousands. They grew from small insignificant acorns that most people never really noticed. They grew at such slow and steady paces that required years and years of consistent patience. They endured the dry seasons and awaited rain with utmost fortitude. They never rushed. Impatience would only have certainly killed them. They fell into deep slumbers in the midst of cold winters, and reawakened again in spring producing buds and blossoms. They were in glory in summer, when they offered their fruits, and then humbled themselves when autumn appeared, shedding their leaves. Trees were never proud or arrogant. They never rebelled or committed mischief. For these reasons, they could outlive generations, after generations of human beings.

An ant, one of the strongest creatures on the planet, relative to its humble size, would try to lift an object heavier than itself. Many times the object would fall, but the ant would keep trying. The ant wouldn't quit. It would keep trying. It was consistent, wise and persistent. How can such tiny creatures, be so wise and determined? How can creatures so insignificant, be so powerful in will and might? Nature was marvelous.

Solomon pondered these very deep questions. He often stared at the stars some nights, wondering where they came from and where they were heading. He realized they came from somewhere, and had to be heading somewhere. Once, he and his mother were sitting alone and Solomon's young curious mind began asking her complex questions about the purpose of human creation.

"Mother, where did people come from?"

"It's hard to say exactly where Solomon," his mother replied. "I can safely tell you that God created us."

"Why?" asked Solomon.

"God is a powerful spirit of love," she said. "He wanted to spread His love. Perhaps He wanted to test His love on us. We are creatures with the ability to think and feel. You see Solomon, God doesn't force us to love Him. He simply asks us to, and we have to make the decision ourselves. No one can force you to love Him. They either do or don't. I guess God created us to know Him, to accept His love and care in our lives and to love Him back."

"So why do people suffer in life and feel pain?" he asked.

"Solomon, it's hard to explain why people suffer or feel pain in life," she said. "Let me ask you this: would you know what happiness felt like, if you first hadn't felt sadness?"

"No I don't think I would know," he said.

"That's the way it is," she said. "A person would never know pleasure, if they never tasted pain. A person would never be satisfied, if they never felt desperation. We must experience the sweet and the sour."

"Sweet and sour?" he repeated.

"Sweet and sour," she said. "If a person doesn't try and taste both flavors, they will never know the difference between the two and never know which is better. Just like light and darkness."

Solomon's mother was wise. She always told him to meet a lot of people. That the more people he knew, the more he would know himself.

Solomon's mother worked in the local village bakery. His father was a teacher. He taught history in the local high school. His father was a strict man, constantly criticizing Solomon about every little thing he did, never acknowledging his own mistakes. His father was the polar opposite of his mother.

At home, Solomon had two older brothers and a

younger sister. As a child, growing up in this household was difficult for Solomon. He was constantly being compared to his brothers, who were always praised for their academic achievements by his father. Solomon got used to hearing the same words from his father, miserably trying to motivate him, but instead, discouraging him.

"You've got to be more like your brothers," His father would constantly say. "They're smarter and better than you and they'll succeed in life. You only want to go outside and play in the field. Your brothers stay home and study hard. They know that if they study hard now, they can play hard later."

These words constantly rang in Solomon's head. It seemed whatever he did, his father would never see or appreciate the person he really was.

Solomon's younger sister was spoiled, but sweet. The family took special care of her, but that didn't bother Solomon, because he loved her. Nevertheless, there were times when Solomon felt left out, and he tried not to let it bother him, but it did. He kept the pain to himself, but it was clear from the look in his eyes that the pain that filled his heart was too much to endure, with rarely anyone taking notice.

Some nights, Solomon would go to his room and

weep silently, not wanting his brothers to hear him cry in fear they would mock him or tell their father.

Solomon's mother was always the empathetic one.
She understood his feelings and would try to lift his spirit. One day, a sobbing Solomon found his mother alone in the kitchen, so he quietly went up to her to console in her.

"Mother, why does father not love me?" he asked while wiping his eyes from tears. "He loves my brothers, but not me. He always tells me how awful I am and how great they are. I never please him. I try to do my best in school, but it's never enough. I am always the one to help him in the fields, while my brothers don't. He hates me, but I don't know what I did."

"Oh honey, wipe your tears," she said. "If you only knew how much I love you. Isn't my love enough? One day Solomon, you'll become someone great. Just be patient and strong. Focus on the positive sides of life, and ignore the negatives. Your father doesn't see the real you. Not everyone will appreciate and love you the same way. You may find a beggar who will treat you as a beggar, but on the other hand, you may find a king who will treat you as a king. It's difficult to find someone who will treat you as a king, but easier to find many who will treat you as a beggar. There are many beggars, but few kings. Be treated as a King by one, rather than be treated as a beggar by a thousand. I know you, the real you! You're my handsome boy, and I love you. Tonight, before you go to sleep, look up at the sky and open your heart. Let the sky fill your heart with love and hope. Look at the sky and open your heart to the Higher Soul."

"What is the Higher Soul?" he asked.

"The Higher Soul created the universe, the planets and the stars," she explained. "The Higher Soul created humans, animals, nature and love. Everything you see, feel and touch, the Higher Soul created. He created all that you see for one purpose."

"What purpose mother?" he asked.

"For the purpose that every creature in existence recognizes and sees Him," she said. "We must acknowledge His power in creation and His eternal love for us. He asks for one thing in return."

"What is it?" he asked.

"He asks us to know Him, appreciate Him and love Him, as He loves us," she explained. "Solomon, learn to love the Higher Soul, and you will find the answer to your life's mysteries and the path to your great destiny. He will guide you. You will never fall, but if you do, He will always be there to break your fall."

"What do I do?" he asked.

"Communicate with Him," she said. "Every night, after midnight and before dawn, talk to the Higher Soul. When no one appreciates who you are, be certain the Higher Soul will."

"What will I say to the Higher Soul?" he asked.

"Whatever you feel you need to say or ask," she said. Just keep your heart open and speak what you feel. "It doesn't matter what you say or ask honey: what matters is that you communicate."

"Why?" he asked.

"Honey, when a human is born, they are born with a power within so great and so strong, that if it was to be set free into the world, it would cause the world to turn over and explode," she said. "An energy so fast, that it could travel to the moon and back quicker than a blink of an eye. That power is locked within us. It is reflected outwards in different ways. Some people reflect that power in the arts like drawing and painting, others in sciences, literatures and in many other ways. Some people reflect that power in hard work and dedication, or in friendship and love. It is the force that drives us to wake up every morning."

Solomon found it difficult to relax. He felt his mind racing. He was nervous. He didn't know what he was going to say to the Higher Soul. He made absolute sure not to talk about it with anyone, certainly not his brothers.

He spent the rest of the day sitting on top of a tree branch in front of his village home. He recalls the many days spent sitting on top of that very tree. It was an old pomegranate tree. He loved eating them.

The inside of a pomegranate contained many seeds, bounded together so sophisticatedly. Some seeds were sweet, while others were sour. Even the outer skin of a pomegranate was used for healing as a medicine. They only grew in warm areas of the world and in the Mediterranean, where they were plentiful.

Solomon sometimes would open a pomegranate and just stare and wonder at how a design could be put together all on its own. He also pondered how a small seed, buried in the soil, could one day become a tree that reaped many fruits and more seeds. Even at such a young age, he understood in his own way, the infinity in creation, or at least a small aspect of it.

He stayed on top of the tree branch until evening. His older brother came out and called his name and told him to come inside, and that it was getting dark. Solomon climbed down and went inside the house.

Midnight had arrived and Solomon was awake. His brothers and sister were asleep. His parents were awake downstairs, having their nightly discussion about what took place that day and other usual matters relating to money and family. Solomon's father was complaining about the poor harvest in the field. He owned an acre of land behind the house. He mainly cultivated oranges, olives and pomegranates.

"The rain has decreased this year," his father said. "I remember in the past when rain was abundant and the harvest was rich. Now, it's not anymore."

People always seemed to compare the past and the present and whatever they compared, it always appeared that the past was always better than the present. Maybe it was because people's expectations were fewer, so whatever came their way, satisfied them.

Nowadays, people were fixated on moments they had had in the past, the friends they had had, the money they had earned and the happiness they had felt. Whereas in the present, they saw fewer friends, earned more money, but were less happy. Maybe the truth was that people were not satisfied with change. People complained about routine and monotonousness, but in fact when change occurred, they preferred the past and the routine.

"I'm disappointed with Solomon," his father said. "He's always unfocused and dreamy. I swear he spends more time sitting on that tree in a day, than he does studying in a month. I'm going to cut that tree down, so he has no place to sit and waste time. He just stares at the sky and thinks. What does he think about?"

"Solomon is different from the others," his mother said. You must understand that. Are all of the fingers on your hand the same length? No, they aren't. So stop comparing Solomon to the other children. He is not them, and they are not him!"

His mother stood up, and walked away in a fury. His father remained seated, indifferent to what she had said. Solomon was in his bed, awake with anticipation. He didn't want to make any noise and wake his siblings. He shared his room with his two older brothers. If they woke, they would certainly hit him or go and tell their father, and Solomon wouldn't want his father to know he was still awake.

He was very nervous about what he was going to say to the Higher Soul that night. He was still unsure what he had to do. He recalled what his mother had said earlier that night. She told him to clear his mind from everything, and look up at the sky, close his eyes and let the voice within speak out.

He could say or ask for anything. He wasn't sure what he wanted. He just wanted to speak to the Higher Soul.

The sky was clear and the moon was a crescent. It was three in the morning. Solomon slowly crept out of bed, and on the tips of his toes, walked across the room, to the window. The stars sparkled in the sky like crystals. A soft wind blew across his face. The white crescent moon shone brightly like a pearl.

A quiet peace went through his body, as never before. A feeling of calm filled his heart. His eyes were fixed on the moon. His inner voice emerged and began to speak.

"Higher Soul, I don't know what to say to You," he said. "I'm Solomon. Where do You come from? I come from here, a village in the mountains. Can I ask You something? Why was I born? My father loves my brothers, but not me. I don't know why. Am I bad? Do You hate me? My mother loves me. She always makes me smile, even when I am too sad to. She tells me that I am special. Am I? She says that one day I will become someone very special. Will I? Can You make me someone special? I want to be loved and needed. I want to make my father love me. Can You do that for me? I want him to be happy, and these days he isn't because his land is dry. Please help my father's land grow a good harvest so he can be happy. My brothers treat me bad and hurt me with words, but I love them. I want to be like them, even if they don't want me around. Please help my brothers, even if they don't want the same for me. Please take care of my baby sister. She's sweet as an angel, and I love her. Please protect my mother and give her the ability to be strong. I want to know many things. Can You give me the power to understand the world around me? I want to understand people, the world and everything, especially the universe. I want to help people, especially the people that are lost, like me. Thank you Higher Soul."

Solomon's inner voice became quiet as his eyes remained fixed at the crescent moon. A light wind blew again, caressing his face. A sense of complete relaxation overtook his body, as he began to feel sleepy. He walked over to his bed, and slipped in, between the sheets. The sheets were warm, and his pillow was soft. He didn't feel alone at the moment. He felt a safe eye looking over him. He took a deep breath, exhaling slowly. He fell asleep.

The morning was glowing. The sun lit up Solomon's room. He woke up, with eyes not fully open. He stretched his arms, across the bed and yawned.

His father was in the kitchen drinking coffee and reading the newspaper. He usually read the newspaper before going to school.

"Good morning Solomon," his father said.

"Good morning father," Solomon responded.

"It's a nice morning today, isn't it son?"

"Yes it is, father."

Solomon's father had never greeted him in the morning before. Most mornings, he would be absorbed in the paper, ignoring everyone and everything around him. This morning was different.

"Solomon, today you and I have a lot of work to do," his father said. "We're going to work on the field, just you and I. I want you ready as soon as you get back from school. While you wait for me to arrive, I want you to start doing your homework,"

"Yes father, I will," replied Solomon.

Solomon ran up the stairs faster than usual in the morning, got dressed and went to school. The school was a twenty-minute walk from his home, so he had to leave a bit early. As he crossed the school yard, he noticed his classmate and friend sitting on the staircase.

"Solomon, how are you?" greeted his friend. "I didn't want to go inside without you, so I decided to wait for you."

"Thanks," said Solomon. "You didn't have to."

His friend's age was identical to his. He lived near by. Often times, they would walk home together. He was his best friend, in fact, his only friend. Living in the village limited his opportunities to meet people and develop new friendships. So, he had to settle for what he could get.

After school, Solomon rushed home, in order to arrive before his father did. He wanted his father to see him doing his homework, and ready to work on the field. Solomon would do anything to please him.

His brothers were in their room, doing their homework. They weren't going to help out with the field work. Usually, it would bother Solomon to be the only one to help his father in the field, while his older brothers stayed indoors, away from the hard labor of field work. This time, it didn't. It was different, at least as far as he could tell.

Solomon's mother was in the kitchen. She was cooking supper. Solomon entered the kitchen, walked up to his mother and kissed her. His mother was pleasantly surprised.

"Thank you Solomon," said his mother. "What was that for?"

"I just love you," he said.

Solomon went to his room and opened a book. He wanted his father to come home and see him studying. Pleasing his father meant so much to him. Solomon took out his math book. The unit he was on was fractions. He began reading the first question that was assigned for homework. As he prepared to answer the question, he heard a knock on the door. It was his father. He had come home from work.

"Where's Solomon?" he asked in a high voice. "Get him down now!"

Solomon heard his father calling for him and came down immediately.

"Let's go," he said. "We've got a lot of farm work to do today,"

Solomon was upset and it was obvious that he was. His head slugged down to the side and his eyes looked straight to the floor. More than anything that day, he wanted his father to see him studying, but his father hadn't even cared to ask.

Solomon followed his father out to the field. He began filling up a bucket with water, and walked around the field, pouring water on the ground, near the root of each tree. Solomon didn't mind doing the work.

Getting outside and being surrounded by nature was something magical to him. Even though he saw the same field and the same trees day after day, he never got grew tired of admiring the power of nature.

The same questions would constantly come to his mind. How could a tree know what to reap? How could a tree know whether to reap apples, and not oranges? How could a tree know to reap olives and not pomegranates?

He knew that olives held miraculous healing powers. He learned from school, that many past civilizations used olive oil to heal.

Solomon continued watering the trees. His father was busy picking out the shrubs that grew around the trees. He was hoping for rain. It hadn't rained for a while. The land was dry. The trees were thirsty. The trees wanted to reap a good harvest, but they needed water. They needed rain water. Rainwater held power from the Higher Soul. Trees grew well when it rained.

The sun in the distance, was beginning to fall below the horizon, and the sky was becoming dark. Solomon had watered all the trees. It was time to go home. Solomon and his father began walking back to the house. They spoke little to each other. All they wanted was to eat, as they were very hungry and tired. They both deserved a meal and rest. They had worked hard that day.

Solomon went inside and his mother greeted him with a smile. Solomon's father entered the house with a frown. An obvious expression displayed by the scrunching of his eyebrows. Nothing seemed to ever satisfy him. No matter what good happened, it was never enough. There was always something to frown about. A pessimist's view of life. On the contrary, were optimists who viewed everything with hope. Solomon's father was certainly a pessimist.

Solomon walked into his room to get changed. His older brother walked in and looked at Solomon in a condescending manner. He had nothing positive to say.

"Solomon, you're filthy and you smell," he said. "Wash up!"

Solomon didn't say a thing. He looked up to his older brother so much, that even when he said such negative things about him, he would believe him. It was obvious that Solomon's brother didn't appreciate what Solomon had done all day. He didn't bother to ask Solomon how many trees he had watered. He didn't even bother to ask Solomon how many mosquitoes had bit him that today. He didn't bother to ask Solomon how many sweat droplets had fallen off his face. He absolutely didn't. He simply discredited Solomon and was quick to mock.

Solomon was hurt. He felt tired and exhausted and now, his brother didn't make him feel any better. Solomon's sister walked into his room.

Solomon's eyes remained fixated at the wall. He recollected a time when he had come home from school and had seen one of his brothers sitting down on the sofa. His brother had looked at him and just smiled. Though it happened so rarely, he still remembered that smile. It brought a feeling of love and joy that day. It was the reassurance of kindness, though his brother showed it so infrequently. What a moment it was!

"How was school Solomon?" asked his brother.

"It was fine," replied Solomon. I had a lot of fun today actually. My teacher gave us pair work and I was paired with a girl I've had a crush on since the beginning of the school year.

"Lucky you," replied his brother. "Is she beautiful?"

"She makes my stomach feel funny," replied Solomon. "I can't explain it. Every morning when I wake up, I can't wait to walk to school just to see her. Every night that passes by, I actually look forward to sleeping so I can see her the next morning. I freeze whenever I'm around her. Her eyes are so bright and her smile makes me want to sing. I remember everything that she says in class. Every time she speaks, I listen closely. Her voice is like music to my ears. I couldn't believe I was paired with her today."

"Did you tell her how you feel?" asked his brother.

"I couldn't," replied Solomon. "I froze again. I couldn't focus on what I was doing. She did most of the work. I just stared at her."

"You'll get another chance little brother," said his brother.

Solomon remembered that conversation with his brother so distinctly. The emotions began to overcome his senses. The pain inside grew larger and larger.

"Why are you crying Solomon?" asked his sister.

"I'm not crying," wept Solomon as he choked back his tears.

"Solomon, why are you sad?" asked his sister.

"I'm not sad, I'm angry," he replied. "I helped father all day in the field, and he didn't even say thanks. Then, our brother comes in the room and tells me how dirty and smelly I am, and that I need to wash up. I hate this family. I'm always ignored and treated badly. What did I do? I never asked for this,"

"Don't be sad Solomon," said his sister. I love you."

Suddenly, those three words made some of Solomon's pain elevate and float away like a cloud. How powerful love can be when it is unconditional. That night, Solomon wanted to speak to the Higher Soul once again.

He wanted to express his thoughts and emotions to the Higher Soul.

The house was still. Everyone was asleep. Solomon stared at the sky. He cleared his mind from all the thoughts that had filled his mind earlier. He focused on the brightest star in the sky. Solomon's inner voice began to speak.

"I hope I can explain my pain to You," said Solomon. "I don't know where to begin. I am only a young boy, but I feel like an old man. I have the body of a young boy, but the mind and heart of a tired old man. I love my mother and obey her completely. I also obey my father without ever objecting, but he doesn't see any good in me. He always compares me to my older brothers, and makes me feel worthless. I can never please him. I am a failure in his eyes. My brothers don't care about me, or my feelings. They're selfish, but my sweet little sister is always kind to me. I don't know what to do. I don't know which way to go. I like school, but my father has already determined my future, as a farmer. My brothers will finish school one day, and travel and see the world. I will be stuck here. I want to see the world too. I want to become the person I'm supposed to become. I want my father to be proud of me and may You allow it to rain abundantly and bless his land so it reaps a good harvest. I hold no animosity or spite inside me towards him in any way. Yes, he hurts me and neglects me, but I have gotten used to that. I also hold no animosity towards my brothers, even though they may hold some towards me. Please, please stand by me, and my family. Show us the way. Guide us and make me a great person. A person who will one day, help the world."

Solomon took a deep breath, and exhaled slowly. He then retreated to his bed. A peace filled Solomon's heart and he felt a comfort that he hadn't felt all day. He sighed with relief. His eyes closed, and he fell asleep.

That night, Solomon had a dream. He saw himself standing on the edge of a mountain, overlooking a sea. He was alone. He wasn't able to move. It was night. He heard a voice behind him, but he couldn't turn to see who or what it was. The voice got louder and nearer, but Solomon could not move or turn his head. The voice got closer and Solomon screamed.

He awoke startled. His heart was racing. He was breathing heavily. His brothers remained asleep and weren't awakened. Solomon was sweating profusely. He hadn't even slept for one hour.

He sat up in bed. He didn't want to sleep again. He tried to recollect the events of the dream he had just had. He was too anxious to look out the window. Something didn't feel right. He could recall the mountain edge in his dream. He recalled being paralyzed, unable to move. He recalled the voice he had heard behind him. He tried to remember what the voice was saying, but couldn't.

He stood up, put on his slippers and walked down the stairs. He didn't want to make any noise, in the fear that his father might wake. His father always seemed to wake up on the wrong side of the bed, always grumpy and irritable.

Solomon tiptoed across the living room. The wooden boards below the floor were creaking. Solomon sat on the sofa and lay back with the lamp on. He felt safer there than upstairs in bed. Light always seemed to bring a sense of safety to a person.

Solomon was drowsy. He cuddled up to the sofa cushion. He stared at the ceiling. He felt comfort. The ceiling reminded him of the sky he liked staring at. He could vaguely remember the dream he had just had. He felt better. That dream terrified him. He fell asleep.

The years passed. The seasons changed. The earth aged. Solomon had grown older. He was in his twenties now. It was winter. The clouds were grey and the sky was heavy. Solomon had just finished working in the field. He thought about his childhood best friend who had finished school with him and was now in some university in a faraway city, continuing his education. Solomon had completed secondary school, but hadn't gone any further. His father didn't think it was necessary for him to do so. He preferred that Solomon become a farmer and not an academic. His brothers had left home. They, too, had traveled away for university.

Over the years, the land had become revived and had reaped rich harvests. The family was living better and more comfortably. Solomon's father was proud of his land and his accomplishments. He believed it was his efforts that had resulted in the land's rich harvest. Little did he realize, if the rain hadn't fallen, the land would have dried up like a raisin, which had once been a moist grape.

Solomon's mother had also been good over the years. She had done everything she could to please the family. Even though pleasing Solomon's father was almost impossible, she still tried the impossible: to please him.

Solomon had grown taller and more handsome. He was still not satisfied. He felt something was missing in his life. There was an urge inside of him, calling out to him.

Through the years, Solomon had lost hope in the Higher Soul. Day by day, he spoke a little less and desired a little less. His sleep hadn't been comfortable. Often times, he would awake suddenly in a panic. The room that was once filled with his brothers was now empty.

It would seem comforting to Solomon that the brothers who had taunted and mocked him for years were finally gone and had left him in peace, but his peace was now filled with an emptiness and a loneliness. He woke to an empty room. He slept in an empty room. The room had become so quiet and lifeless.

He missed his brothers. He missed them even though they had hurt him. He only wanted life back in his room. He wanted life back in his home.

His parents had become quiet and still. They were older now and less desiring of the needs of this life. When people desired something from life, they seemed more animated and alive. On the other hand, when people no longer desired anything from life, they seemed indifferent to everything and apathetic.

Solomon was slowly becoming this way. He felt no purpose, no reason to want anything. He sat on his bedside and stared as if in a daze. His sister walked in.

"What are you staring at Solomon?" she asked.

Solomon didn't respond. His sister asked again. Solomon didn't respond, but then he slowly turned his head to the side and looked at her.

"Do you miss them?" he asked.

"Miss who?" she asked.

"Miss them, you know who," he said.

"You mean our brothers?" she said. "Yes, I do. Do you miss them?"

Solomon said nothing and turned his head back to the wall, where he had been staring before.

"I don't know what to do," Solomon confessed as he confided in his sister. "I don't know what I am supposed to do with my life. I was born a farmer, but this wasn't my choice. I love farming, but I don't want to surrender my life to it. Our brothers are traveling and meeting other people. Why can't I? Why can't I decide who I want to be? Why does father oblige me to work on the farm when I prefer to travel? I know how to farm, but there are so many things I don't know how to do. I don't know how to speak a different language. I don't know how to play a musical instrument. I don't know how to read a compass. All I know is how to harvest and gather crops. I want to see the world a bit more before I decide to stay in one place. I wake up every day seeing the same land and seeing the same sky. I want to see the sky from another place. I want to stand on the land of other people. I don't want to die a farmer. I want to live a farmer among many other things."

CHAPTER 2 - THE DREAM

Solomon felt a bit of relief after confiding in his sister. He felt more clarity. It was helpful for him to express his pain and anger, allowing his body and his mind to discharge. She was his friend, someone emotionally close to him that he trusted and depended on, unconditionally. She was always loyal and supportive of him.

He felt more focused and aware of his pain and what was really bothering him. He wanted his life to change. That night, he felt the need to talk to the Higher Soul. It had been months since even the thought of it had come to mind. He was in need of the Higher Soul more than ever before.

That night, he recalled the first time he had ever spoken to the Higher Soul. He recalled the passion inside of him to live, and how he had had to whisper in fear of waking his elder brothers. His brothers were not there anymore.

They had gone away to find their own passions in life. Solomon was happy for them.

The night, the sky and the stars gave him a hope and an optimism he hadn't felt in a long time. He felt more alive that night. He wondered how people could go through their days, weeks, months and years, not ever noticing the sky at night.

The wind was chilly. Winters were often warm in the Mediterranean, but from time to time, the wind blew slightly colder and would bring a chill into the house. It didn't bother him that night. Solomon had the window wide open. He could see the field. The land had been reaping better harvests as the years had passed. He remembered when he was fourteen, asking the Higher Soul to bless the land and to allow the clouds above to shower the land, so that it could reap a good harvest.

His father was more pleased with the land than ever before. His brothers were away studying. His mother and sister were well. He was suddenly questioning whether or not that night had made all the changes take place. Then again, Solomon didn't get what he asked for. He recalled asking for his father's pride and to become someone that one day all people would recognize and adore.

He recalled asking for the power of understanding the universe and the inner beings of humans. He remembered every detail of that night. Solomon's inner voice began to speak.

"Why have You forgotten me?" he asked. "Why? I depended on You, but now I feel there is no one to depend on. I walk a path I do not understand. I walk a path I did not choose. I wake every morning with a sigh of distress and discomfort. I know I should be somewhere else, but I don't know where that place is. I know I should be someone else, but I don't know who that person is. I want to know. I need to know."

As Solomon's inner voice spoke out to the Higher Soul, he got a glimpse of the sky and wondered how long it had been since he had looked up at it. How relieved it made him. He knew in his heart that some place better awaited him. He continued to speak.

"I want my pain to go away," he confessed. "I ask You to relieve my loneliness and confusion and set me on a path of direction and joy. I don't know how to begin, but I want to. Show me a sign. Show me a way. Show me a flicker of light that can set me on the path. I wait for that sign. I will keep my eyes and heart open. I know, deep down inside, that I was meant for something greater"

Solomon felt a relief once again. He felt a relief and comfort after the expulsion of his inner distress, because he felt he was no longer alone. He felt that the Higher Soul understood him and was going to guide him.

That night he slept comfortably again. The comfort he felt couldn't be compared to all the gold in the world.

Solomon fell asleep and began to dream. In his dream, he found himself standing in the middle of his father's field. Darkness filled the sky. He could not see clearly or hear anything. He called out in a loud tone.

"Father!" he called out. "I'm here! Mother, I'm here! I'm here!

Solomon heard no answer. Fear filled his heart. The darkness overtook his senses. He could not see, hear or feel a thing around him. He could not move. He tried to walk, but was unable to do so.

"Is anyone here?" he asked in terror. "I can't move! I can't see! Help me! Father! Mother!"

Suddenly, Solomon woke in a puddle of sweat. His heart pounded harder and harder with each breath he took. He called out to his father, but to no avail. His mother heard him yell out and immediately ran into his room.

"What's wrong honey?" she asked. "What's wrong? Did you have a bad dream?"

"I don't know," he answered in a panic. "I don't know where I was. I don't know where I was. I was standing in the field, or at least I thought I was. It was dark. So dark! So quiet! I could hear nothing. I yelled out for father, but he didn't answer me. I yelled out for you, but you didn't answer me. I felt alone, so alone mother. I was so scared."

Solomon's mother embraced him.

"Solomon my dear, don't be afraid," she said. "You have done nothing wrong to cause this fear. Dreams are sometimes good, and sometimes bad. You can't control what you see, but you can try to understand what they mean. You know, dreams can be interpreted. They have meanings. They are signs from the Higher Soul. They are guides and sometimes, warnings. Why they come at certain times for some people is unclear, but they are definitely messages. How else could the Higher Soul communicate with us?"

"Who can interpret dreams mother?" he hastily asked.

"Solomon, we are told the story of a great human with a great power, that lived in ancient times," she began to recount. "This story is believed to be true by the people of the three great faiths: Judaism, Christianity and Islam.

"Are they the same?" he asked.

"Well, they all believe in the Higher Soul," she

said. "So yes, they are the same. Let me tell you this tale. It's about a boy named Joseph. He was a handsome young boy, just like you. He had many brothers. His father was called Jacob, and he was a man of faith and had a strong connection to the Higher Soul. Joseph was one of the youngest children in the family. Jacob loved Joseph very much. He was his favorite son and he was very protective of him. Joseph's older brothers noticed the special care and attention given to Joseph by their father and so, were very jealous of him. They despised him and were very angry because they knew that their father loved him the most above them all. One day, Joseph's father sent him out to find his brothers, who were tending sheep. Jacob wanted Joseph to bring back word as to how his brothers were faring. When the brothers spotted Joseph, they plotted to kill him. With an emotional change of heart, one of Joseph's brothers could not bear to see Joseph die, so he suggested they sell Joseph to the first caravan that passed by. He also suggested they kill an animal and cover Joseph's coat with its blood, to confuse their father and have him believe he had been killed by a wild animal."

"What's a caravan mother?" Solomon asked.

"A caravan is a group of desert merchants," she said. "They often traveled on camels. They traded different items such as food, animals and even human slaves in ancient times. Let's get back to the story. That particular path that Joseph and his brothers were on was often crossed by caravans. Joseph's brothers threw him in a pit while they waited for one. They could hear Joseph crying down below. Some of them began to regret what they had done, but the others didn't. They hated Joseph because he was loved the most by their father. A caravan was passing along and the oldest brother spoke to the caravan guide. He made a sale and sold his brother to him. Joseph was lifted up and taken away. He was now a slave. Joseph's brothers ran home in distress and told their father that Joseph had been killed by a wild animal. Jacob became so sad that he began to cry. He cried for years and years. His pain was too overwhelming. Joseph's brothers were tormented. The very sight of their father and the pain he was enduring only left them in more grief and misery. They tried to look for Joseph, but Joseph was gone. Joseph had been taken to a far away place. He was taken to Egypt where he was sold to an Egyptian advisor to the king. Joseph became significant to his master. The years passed and Joseph grew more in rank and influence. One day, Joseph was in his master's home and the wife of his master saw him. She saw Joseph's physical beauty and wanted Joseph to embrace her. Joseph, a man of honor refused and told her that he was loyal to his master and would not break that trust. Upset with Joseph, the wife of his master called the guards and had Joseph imprisoned. Joseph was upset, but his faith in the Higher Soul kept him hopeful. Seven years passed and Joseph remained in prison. One day, two prison mates of Joseph's were bothered by dreams that they had had the night before. Joseph offered his interpretations for both of them. One of the prisoners was told by Joseph that he would be released and would serve the king of Egypt in his court. The other prisoner was told that he would die shortly thereafter. The interpretations were absolutely correct and one of the prisoners was released and served in the king of Egypt's court while the other was killed. Years passed and Joseph remained in prison. His faith kept his soul guided. One night, the king of Egypt was awakened by a dream that was surely a nightmare. The king dreamed the same dream for a year. That dream terrified the king. It drove him mad. He could not sleep. He could not think. He could not live. One day, he stood up and offered a life of wealth and power to anyone that could interpret his dream. At that moment, the man that had been imprisoned with Joseph for several years spoke to the king of Egypt and told him of Joseph's great power. Joseph was summoned to the court and the king of Egypt asked Joseph to interpret his dream. Joseph did. He told the king that Egypt would be blessed with seven years of prosperity to be followed by seven years of famine. With that said the king of Egypt believed Joseph and made him his highest official. Joseph was in charge of collecting all food to be used during the years of famine. When the famine came, the Egyptians were able to survive. Joseph's interpretation saved the Egyptians. One day during the famine, Joseph's brothers came to Egypt to request supplies from Joseph himself, but were not aware that Joseph was their long lost brother who had now become a great official in the Egyptian kingdom. Joseph's eyes watered with sadness, but he remained in control. He asked them what they wanted and they requested food supplies. Joseph told them that in order for them to get the supplies they needed, they would first need to bring their father to Egypt. They did, and when his father appeared, Joseph revealed himself to them. They reconciled and Jacob moved his entire family to Egypt and settled with Joseph."

Solomon's eyes were illuminated with wonder. As he heard the story, he could only imagine that he was Joseph and the exciting journey Joseph took was indeed awaiting him. This story brought Solomon to life.

"Now, you can go back to sleep Solomon," said his

mother.

"I love you mother," he said.

Solomon lay back and concentrated his thoughts on the story his mother had just told him. He wondered how the life of Joseph compared to his own life. Joseph had brothers that despised him and were envious of him, and Solomon too had brothers that didn't treat him so well. Joseph was handsome and cherished by his father, while Solomon was also handsome and was dearly loved by his mother. Joseph could interpret dreams and communicate with the Higher Soul. Perhaps one day, he too would be able to interpret dreams.

Suddenly, a thought crossed Solomon's mind. He was different from Joseph. He was fixated on the difference that Joseph's father loved Joseph with all his heart. He loved him so much that he would have given up his own life to save Joseph's. He would have sacrificed the world to make sure Joseph was safe and sound. Solomon didn't feel that love from his father. Solomon's father rarely noticed him throughout the day, and if he did, it was unintentional. Other times, Solomon's father would only notice Solomon when he needed his help on the farm or to run an errand for him. Other than that, his father couldn't care less where Solomon was or what he was doing.

What hurt Solomon the most was that it was his father. If a random person had taken advantage of him, he wouldn't have minded so much, but having his own father take advantage of him was painful, because love was supposed to prevent that.

Solomon was beginning to understand that some people, no matter what you did for them, would never be appreciative or grateful. He began to understand that, when people wanted to succeed in life and get ahead, they didn't need to step on someone else's head to do so. If his father had shown him a little gratitude and appreciation, he would have loved him more and would have wanted to help him unconditionally. Nevertheless, a man could always change his destiny.

Solomon was thinking. Joseph wasn't appreciated by his brothers, but he became an official to the king of Egypt. Solomon wasn't appreciated by his father, but he could also become someone.

The moon shone bright that night. The field was glowing from the radiance of the moonlight. Solomon fell asleep. He began to dream.

He found himself in a desert, walking along. It was an unknown place. The sand hills were wide. The sun was bright and scorching the land. Solomon saw a human figure in the distance. The figure was difficult to describe. The heat blurred Solomon's vision. He began to walk towards it. As he walked, his feet formed prints in the sand below. The figure stopped and turned to face Solomon. Suddenly, the figure began to wave and gesture for Solomon to come closer. Solomon began to run. As he ran, the figure got farther away, while waving its arms. He began to yell to the figure, but the figure was too far away. The sky stretched along the horizon. The land was barren. The figure suddenly disappeared. A great fear gripped Solomon. He made complete turns, but saw no one, only the sand that seemed to stretch forever.

Solomon awoke. It was morning. The remnants of his dream remained vivid. The sun was bright and shone on his face. He could not understand what the dream meant, but wondered if the story of Joseph his mother had told him had any influence on what he saw.

He got out of bed and went outside through the front door and took a look at the road across from the house. From time to time, people were seen walking across the road, but Solomon never knew where they were going. Solomon's father was in the back, watering the fields. A windy chill passed through Solomon's body as he recalled the dream and the figure in the desert. He couldn't remember if the figure had said anything to him.

The day passed and the night came again. Solomon was anxious to sleep again, awaiting another dream, another message. Solomon stood by the window and looked up at the sky. The stars were too numerous to count. Solomon began to wonder about their creation. He remembered what he had learned from science class. Stars were big masses of gas in space that generated energy. They came in different sizes. They were points of light in the dark sky and guides for humans. He knew they were more than what he had learned in science class.

Solomon felt a bit jealous of them, because of their freedom. He was also jealous because the stars knew what they were and where they were supposed to be. Stars knew their destinies and even the moon did. It knew the purpose for its existence: that it had to orbit around the earth. It knew that because the Higher Soul had told it. The sun had a purpose. Without the sun's heat and light, life wouldn't exist on the earth. All creatures on the earth depended on the sun for its heat and light.

He knew that feeling of being needed and depended on was wonderful. Solomon just like the sun, wanted to be needed and depended on: perhaps not for heat and light, but maybe for something else. He, too, wanted a purpose. The

Higher Soul ordained the stars, the moon and the sun to their destinies, but maybe Solomon was forgotten. He may have to discover his own purpose. If that was true, then Solomon could be anything he wanted.

Solomon felt more optimistic. His inner voice began to speak.

"Higher Soul," he called out. "I want to be as the stars in the universe, as the moon when it is full and radiant, and as the sun, when it shines its glorified light on the earth. I, too, want to be great, to serve the universe somehow. I want to see the world and meet many kings and priests. I want to be as the stars, the soon and the sun are."

Solomon began to yawn. He pulled the blanket down half way and slipped into bed. He covered his feet and body. He felt relaxed. He was looking forward to seeing another dream and sign. He was on the path to something good, he felt. It took a while for Solomon to fall asleep. Often times, excitement could deprive a person of sleep, as could fear. Solomon fell into a deep sleep.

A dream commenced. Solomon was in his room. It was as if he wasn't asleep at all. Was he awake? Was he dreaming? Solomon walked across the room in slow motion. Everything around him was moving in slow motion. He stared out his bedroom window; it was still night time. He looked down and saw a tree glowing that he had never seen before. He focused on the tree. Suddenly, the same figure in his past dream was sitting next to the tree. Solomon couldn't move. His fear overtook him. The figure didn't move. It said nothing. Solomon couldn't speak or move. The figure began to climb the tree until it reached the top branch. It stood up on the branch and faced Solomon. Solomon began to feel a fear he hadn't felt before. The figure spoke.

"Before you run, learn to walk," it said, then vanished.

Solomon woke in panic and terror. He got up, too afraid to look outside the window. He was afraid the figure was out there waiting for him. He turned on the light in his room. The light brought a little comfort. The words of the figure were echoing in his mind. He pondered the meaning of these words. Solomon already knew how to walk and run. The words kept repeating themselves over and over again in his mind. His head began to throb with pain. He was still very afraid and anxious and that immobilized him.

The light of dawn began to crack the sky in half. Solomon didn't return to bed. He kept repeating the words over and over again. He was going to understand the words literally, as he could think of no other way to understand them.

It was early in the morning. The morning sun hadn't quite risen yet. It was the beginning of a new day and a new start. Solomon decided to heed the words he had heard in his dream and go for a walk. It had been a long time since he had done that.

The morning was chilly. Solomon got dressed and left the house quietly. As he was leaving, his sister awoke

"Solomon, where are you going?" she asked.

This was strange for Solomon's sister, as she had never seen him wake so early to leave the house, except when he had school.

"I'm going for a walk," he said. "I'll be back in a while."

Solomon opened the back door of the house and stepped outside. The sounds of birds in the sky filled the air. Solomon enjoyed the singing. In the distance, a thick mist hovered over the land, something common during the Mediterranean winters.

Solomon's breath was visible as he exhaled. He looked at the road in front of his home. He wondered what lay along the road. He couldn't remember the last time he had walked along the road that was so near, offering many directions. He wondered how many people like him lived somewhere and didn't even know what surrounded them.

Solomon walked across the front garden and reached the road. The road, which he hadn't noticed for ages, was now going to be traveled.

He began walking. The trees that lined the sides of the road were many. Birds were everywhere: in the trees, in the sky and on the ground. The sun was beginning to rise over the horizon. The colors of the sky were varied. He had no idea where he was heading, but he knew he had to walk. He knew the road ahead would lead him somewhere eventually.

A simple walk along the road was becoming an intriguing discovery for Solomon. It was like discovering an uncharted island, where everything was new: a new world, with every step he took, which felt newer and more intriguing. The leaves on the trees vibrated softly.

Up ahead in the distance, Solomon noticed a man walking along with a mule. Solomon got closer and approached the man by politely greeting him. The man smiled back and greeted Solomon.

"Hello young man," said the man. "Where are you from?"

"I'm from here," Solomon said. "My home is two hundred meters behind."

"I haven't seen you before," said the man. "I have

walked this road many years with my mule. I'm a merchant. I buy products from the city and sell them to shops in surrounding villages."

"You're a merchant?" Solomon asked. "I've never seen a merchant with a mule. What kind of merchant are you?"

"Well young friend, it's easy to judge someone by his appearance," he replied. "You look at me and see a man with a mule. You don't know where I come from or if I am poor or rich. You don't know if I am educated or ignorant. You simply see a man with a mule. It's not your fault. Most people are this way. They see the outer shell of things and never take the time to see the inner qualities."

Solomon didn't respond, but listened carefully.

"I'm a merchant and I'm rich," he said. "I choose to deliver my goods by mule, because I believe when something in life works well, there is no need to change it. My mule has never broken down on me. It has never disobeyed me, betrayed me or turned its back on me. It is loyal to me, so I am loyal to it. If I were to turn my back on my mule, than I would turn my back on everything and everyone. Loyalty and trust are the bases to any relationship, whether in friendship or business. My mule is a friend, because it is loyal."

Solomon was beginning to understand something he had never understood before. This was the first time he learned about trust, or that mules make loyal friends. The merchant and the mule continued to walk. Solomon walked along.

"Where are you heading?" asked the merchant.

"Nowhere," said Solomon. "I'm only walking."

"Only walking?" asked the merchant. Are you exercising?"

"No, I'm not," said Solomon. "I am only walking."

"How long are you walking for?" asked the merchant.

"I am not sure how long or where I am heading," said Solomon. "All I know is that this is the first time in a long time that I walk on this road and whatever I see or do, will be a new experience for me. Also, I've been told that in order to run, I must learn to walk."

"These are wise words," the merchant said. "You can understand these words literally in that a baby can never learn to walk if it first doesn't learn to crawl. A child can never learn to run if it first doesn't learn to walk. Life has steps to climb before a person can reach his desired level. Before a merchant can ever learn to trade, he must first learn to buy and sell products. He must understand and learn the market and the demands of the market. He must learn to socialize and convince buyers to buys the goods he is providing. Learning to walk is a metaphor my young friend. Before you see the world, see what surrounds your very home."

They arrived at a small shop in a neighboring village.

Would you like to see me make a sale?" the merchant asked.

"Yes, I would," said Solomon.

The merchant approached a shop. The shop sold food products and kitchen utensils. The merchant uncovered his goods that were hanging from the mules back. Many products were hanging such as utensils, sponges, soaps and chocolates.

As the man approached the shopkeeper, Solomon couldn't stop staring at the mule. He was amazed how obedient the mule was. Who knows how many kilometers the mule walked, or how much weight it carried on its back? Nevertheless, it kept moving and never stopped. It kept moving, and the more it moved, the stronger it became. Solomon saw wisdom in the mule.

The shopkeeper made a purchase and the merchant bade him goodbye and thanked him.

"That's how you make a sale, young friend," said the merchant.

"Very impressive," said Solomon.

"This is what I do," said the merchant. "I make sales. Every sale I make pushes me to make another. I never look too far ahead, only one sale at a time. If I look too far ahead, I'll ignore the sale in front of me."

CHAPTER 3 - THE TRUTH

Solomon and the merchant continued to walk along the road. Another shop soon appeared. The merchant made another sale and felt more satisfied. It was noon and the sun was bright.

"Tell me about yourself," said the merchant.

"What do you want to know?" replied Solomon. "I'm no one special."

"On the contrary, young friend," he said. "You're a young man with a vision. I can feel it. You're on a road, on a path to someplace where you can find yourself. You can be what you want to be. All you have to do is ask."

The words of the merchant, sounded like the words of his mother. He recalled his mother's wise words, when she had said that whatever he wanted to do or to be in life, all he had to do was look up at the sky and ask the Higher

Soul.

"You see young friend, everyone in life can choose his path," he said. "He can be and do whatever he wants. At first, he has to believe in it, and want it more. Second, he must ask God to guide him to it and third, he must strive and put effort into getting it. A man cannot simply ask and wait on the side. He must plan and execute. Also, one very important thing to remember is that you must watch out for signs. God will guide you with signs. Keep your eyes open. You may meet someone coincidently or see something that shows you the way."

"When you say God, do you mean the Higher Soul?" asked Solomon.

"Well, you can call God whatever you want," he said. "You can call Him God, the Higher Soul, Supreme Being, the Divine, Yahweh, Adonai, Jehovah, the Father or Allah. It doesn't matter what you call Him. What's important is that you call on Him."

Solomon was becoming more convinced of signs and that the Higher Soul communicated in this way. It was no coincidence that he had had a dream that had ordered him to walk, and by walking, he would meet a merchant and his mule, and that this merchant would know the secrets of the universe.

They continued walking. Solomon looked back to see how far he had been walking. At this point, he didn't mind the walk or the interesting conversation with the man and his mule.

"My young friend, what do you do in life?" asked the merchant.

"It's hard to say," said Solomon. "I'm not sure what I do. I work on a farm with my father. I finished secondary school. I guess that's it.

"May I ask you a question, young friend?" asked the merchant.

"Yes, please do," answered Solomon.

"What do you want to do in life?" asked the merchant.

Solomon was stunned by the question. Never had anyone in his life asked him such a direct and honest question. His own father, that he had lived with all his life never took a minute to ask him this simple but powerful and striking question. Solomon was at a loss for words. He couldn't answer the question.

"I'm not sure what I want to be," answered Solomon.

"Well, young friend," said the merchant. "That was the answer I was looking for. You see, no one really knows who he wants to be or what he wants to do in life. The person discovers it suddenly. There is no manual for living life. You make your own manual. Answers do not always come prepared with every question. Sometimes, you must keep your eyes open to the signs and live for the day. The answers will come, eventually."

Solomon was most pleased by the man's wise words. He always yearned for some wisdom and truth. He yearned for logical guidance and rationality and yearned even more for the spirituality that guided the soul. Solomon was beginning to understand the purpose. He was beginning to understand the truth.

"I think I have to turn back now, Sir," said Solomon. "It's getting late and I am getting far from home."

"No worries, my young friend," said the merchant. "It was a pleasure meeting you. You are more than welcome to join me every morning. I make my deliveries every morning at the same time."

"Why every morning?" asked Solomon.

"Well, it gives me a reason to wake up in the morning," said the merchant. "We all need a reason to wake up in the morning,"

"Well, I might just take you up on that offer," said Solomon.

"I will be on this road, at exactly the same time and place you saw me today," said the merchant. "Join me. I can use a young friend and helper. I'll even pay you. You might also learn a thing or two."

"I will think about it," said Solomon. "By the way, do you have a name?"

"It's Abraham. My name is Abraham."

"I'm Solomon."

"It's nice to meet you Solomon," said Abraham.

"Nice to meet you too." said Solomon.

As they parted, Abraham began to hum a melody while pulling his mule along. Perhaps being a traveling merchant had allowed him to find ways of entertaining himself, especially on those lonely days and nights.

Solomon began walking back. There was no way of getting lost, since he had only walked in one direction. He walked passed the shops where Abraham had done business. He was surprised that the shops were located in the area. He had never walked this way before.

He decided to run lightly, so he could arrive home sooner. As he ran, the wind blew in his face. He felt invigorated and alive. What a day it was. A simple walk had turned out to be something more fascinating and had produced a day filled with stories and exploration.

Solomon slowed down as he got closer to his home.

His father was strolling around the farm, and it looked like he hadn't even noticed that Solomon had been gone all day. As Solomon approached, his father took notice of him. Solomon's father waved for him to come over.

"Where have you been all day Solomon?" asked his father.

"I went for a walk," Solomon said. "I woke up early in the morning and decided to walk.

"Since when do you wake up early in the morning to walk?" asked his father.

"Since this morning." he replied.

His father wasn't pleased with Solomon's response.

"So, while I was working on the farm, you were out walking and wasting time?" asked his father.

"Well father, with all due respect," said Solomon. "Time is spent differently by different people. You may find walking a waste of time, but I may not. On the other hand, you may find farming a good way of spending your time, but I may find it a waste of time. We are two different people. We see things differently."

His father was startled by his response. Never had he heard Solomon speak this way to him before. Most of the time, Solomon either said nothing, or walked away with his head lowered to the ground. This time it was different.

"Who taught you to disrespect me by speaking this way?" asked his father.

"No one father," said Solomon. "I learned how to speak this way on my own and I would never disrespect you. I just simply have an opinion now".

"The next time you decide to go for a walk, I must be informed," said his father. "Do you understand?"

"I understand father," said Solomon. "I'll inform you. As a matter of fact, I am going for a walk again tomorrow morning. Don't expect me back until late noon or early evening."

"What about the farm?" asked his father. "You have work to do on the farm."

"I have work to do on myself, father," Solomon replied.

"No you don't," said his father. "You have work to do on the farm and that's an order."

"Is that all you see me as, father?" asked Solomon. "Is that all you think I am capable of? Farming is a wonderful career and I know that. It requires a healthy body, a healthy mind, determination and intelligence. This is what you have chosen for me, but you have never asked me what

I wanted. All of my life, you have limited me. You have told me that I wasn't good enough to do anything else: that I was a failure. Why? You supported my brothers and sent them away to university, so that they could become and achieve something greater. As for me, you never supported me and always neglected me. Was I not smart enough to continue my studies? Was I not smart enough to make something of myself? I am beginning to understand the world now father. There is no need to convince me of your ways. I am learning the ways of the world. I am not asking you to teach me. The world will. I only ask you for your support and love. That's all, father. I need nothing else. I am your son."

His father was at a loss for words. Once again, never had he imagined Solomon would speak this way.

"Father, I have found a job," said Solomon. "I will work as a merchant. I have been given an opportunity I cannot refuse. This opportunity will allow me to travel around the area, meet new people and learn new skills. I will deal with money, learn to sell and purchase goods, learn to convince and attract customers and become more aware of the world."

"God bless you, my son," said his father. "This is what I have always wanted to see from you; determination and ambition. Go, travel and learn. You have my love and support. Know that every evening when you come home, dinner will be waiting for you."

For the first time in Solomon's young life, he had looked upon his father's eyes and seen proud eyes. Solomon felt a power inside him burn and a determination grow like never before. He was excited about the journey ahead and his new job as a traveling merchant. How amazing that a dream relayed a simple message that became a path to a journey that would change his life forever!

Solomon felt more confident in himself and more aware of his capabilities. His mother and sister heard the news and were pleasantly surprised. What a change in a mere day! Yesterday had given no indication of what happened today.

Solomon went to his room and got changed for dinner. The table was awkwardly quiet. Solomon's father didn't speak. His mother was slowly putting food into her mouth, while keeping a lowered gaze.

"So, where are you going to work Solomon?" asked his sister.

"I'm not sure exactly," said Solomon. "Everywhere, I suppose."

"What will you do?" asked his sister.

"Well, I will be working as a traveling merchant,"

said Solomon. "I will travel from shop to shop, from village to village selling products."

"What kind of products?" asked his mother.

"Products for home," said Solomon. "Such as sponges, utensils, soaps and some food items."

"How much money will you be earning?" asked his father.

"Well, I haven't discussed it yet with the merchant," said Solomon. "I assume I will earn what I sell."

"Let's hope you don't get taken advantage of," replied his father.

"Father, whatever happens, this will give me a chance to build my character," said Solomon. "Can't you see that? Before you run, you must learn to walk."

"What nonsense are you speaking of, walking before you run?" questioned his father.

"It's not nonsense, father," said Solomon. "It's not nonsense at all. How can I learn anything if I don't take the first step? How can I learn a language if I don't study the alphabet first? I cannot jump too far if my legs have never been trained to land."

"How did you get so smart Solomon?" asked his mother.

"I'm your son, aren't I?" replied Solomon

That night, Solomon planned out the morning. He was to get up before dawn to say a prayer to the Higher Soul, a prayer for guidance.

Solomon felt exhausted from walking all day. That night, he had a dream. Solomon was standing behind the seashore overlooking the darkened sea. The crescent moon above glowed, and only a few stars could be seen behind the shifting clouds. The waves were strong. They made a sound that rocked the air. The tides could be seen rolling in and crashing into the shore. Solomon was standing behind the edge of the shore. In the distance, a small boat rocked side to side with a human figure inside. The figure stood inside the boat and stared at Solomon. Solomon focused his sight. The figure stared.

"Hello. Are you alright?" Solomon yelled.

The figure remained fixedly staring at Solomon. Solomon climbed down the rocks and walked closer to the shore. As he got closer, the figure became clearer. The waves got stronger. The wind was heavy and the sky was getting darker. Solomon was close and the figure stood staring.

"Who are you?" Solomon asked.

The figure did not reply.

"Who are you?" asked Solomon again.

The clouds above cleared and the moonlight shone brighter below. Solomon could see the figure's face. It was a female. The girl looked very familiar. Suddenly, a sound rumbled across the waves and the boat stood still as the girl spoke.

"Solomon, read my soul," she said.

Solomon woke in a panic. The dream was vivid. It was almost certainly real. Solomon was confused. Questions filled his mind. What did she mean by reading her soul? Solomon was bewildered. Solomon stood by the window. He raised his hands to the sky and said a prayer to the Higher Soul. He was more certain than ever that the Higher Soul was listening to every prayer and was responding.

While he lay in bed, he recalled the sea and the crescent moon he had seen in his dream. He recalled the boat that rocked side to side and the girl he had seen inside it. He closed his eyes and fell asleep again.

The day was dawning. Solomon got up on his feet and stretched his arms over his head. The sun hadn't crossed over the horizon yet. He washed his face and brushed his teeth. He got dressed and walked over to the staircase. He wanted to walk down the stairs as quietly as possible so as not wake up any members of his family. His sister was a light sleeper and could always sense when Solomon woke.

"You're going to work?" asked his sister.

Solomon smiled and nodded his head in affirmation.

"Good luck," said his sister.

Solomon smiled again and waved good-bye. As he was walking down the steps, he motioned to his sister that he would see her later that today. His sister smiled.

"Bring me back something," she said.

Solomon smiled again. He knew his sister well. Ever since she was a child, pleasing her wasn't difficult at all, as long as you brought her a gift or something sweet to eat. He winked at her, gesturing that he would bring her something back with him.

He reached the back door and unlocked the door knob. He turned the knob and the door opened. The door made a sound as it slowly began to open. He felt the cool air seep through under the door. As the door opened fully, the sight was graceful. Birds danced around above the land, the clouds shape shifted across the sky and the colors of the horizon were breathtaking. He walked across the field and reached the road. He looked in both directions and could not see anyone. He began walking in the same direction as he had done the day before. He walked fifty meters before spotting Abraham and the mule. Abraham was sitting down on the side of the road, eating.

"Good morning, young friend," said Abraham.

"Good morning," replied Solomon.

"I'm glad to see that you've decided to join me," Abraham said. "Please sit down and eat with me. It's not much, only bread and olives, but it will surely satisfy your morning appetite."

"I will try it," said Solomon. "I don't usually eat breakfast."

"You're wrong not to," said Abraham. "Breakfast is the most important meal of the day. To eat a little is better like some bread, olives or cheese. It's light, healthy and very delicious."

Solomon joined Abraham for breakfast. The mule stood quietly. The bread was warm and the olives were bitter as they usually were and very oily.

"Olive oil is very healthy for you young friend," said Abraham.

"Really?" asked Solomon. "I didn't know that."

Solomon had been surrounded by olives all of his life, but knew little about the benefits they yielded. Abraham continued to speak.

"In history, we are told the olive tree was a symbol of power and holiness," Abraham said. "In Greek mythology, there lived a very powerful queen named Athena. She was the favorite daughter of the god Zeus. He loved her so much that he gave her his shield. On that shield, there were images of the head of Medusa, his buckler and the thunderbolt, his weapon. She had a temple called the Parthenon. It was in Athens, Greece, not too far from here where we are now. According to myths and legends, the temple became hers as a result of one thing: she offered a gift of the olive tree to the Athenian people.

Another story we are told is about the ancient Olympic Games. Now, the ancient Greeks had four great national festivals, but the most famous were the Olympic Games. The ancient Olympic Games took place every four years in the summer. They were held at Olympia, in the sanctuary of the god Zeus. One very famous competition was called the pentathlon, which was a series of five events. The events were javelin hurling, wrestling, long jumping, discus throwing and sprinting. In the closing event, a race run in armor took place. Here is what is very interesting again about the olive. The winners of this competition were awarded crowns of wild olive."

Solomon was fascinated once again with the knowledge Abraham had. He felt more and more enlightened.

"You know so much," said Solomon.

"I know what I know from what I learn, hear and read," said Abraham. "I learn by meeting new people and listening to what they have learned. I also learn by traveling and seeing new places. Reading alone cannot make a person knowledgeable. One can read a thousand books, but learn nothing. A knowledgeable person knows this and acquires knowledge from all sources. Knowledge is power. The more you know, the more powerful you become."

Breakfast was over and they both took sips of water before heading off. They walked down the road. They made their first stop at the same shop they had visited the day before. The shopkeeper bought a few products. They made their way to the next shop. The clouds were heavy, almost ready to pour rain. At the next shop, Solomon was allowed to make a sale. As he entered the shop, the shopkeeper looked surprised at Solomon.

"Young man," said the shopkeeper. "I haven't seen you around here before. Are you the merchant's son?"

"No, no sir," said Solomon. "I'm not his son. I work for him. In fact, I just began today. I live around here, not too far away, just above the road about two hundred meters from here."

"Well, it's good to see a young face around here

working," the shopkeeper said. "I appreciate a young man that works hard to build his life. When I was your age, I worked for a shopkeeper and I remember working hard and never complaining. As the years went on, I became more experienced in the business and then a few years later, I opened my own shop. When I opened my own shop, I felt like a man. I was responsible for myself and able to control a business. Now, I own three shops and I still haven't complained. A man builds himself brick by brick."

Solomon offered the man the products he was selling. The shopkeeper took some sponges, soaps and dried foods. Solomon felt good. He felt proud of himself. He even made a little profit and was allowed to keep it. The money he made, however little, was great wealth in his eyes. He looked into his hands and didn't even bother counting the coins, but he knew the first sale was the most important one. However small the first sale was, the next one would be bigger.

Solomon and Abraham continued on their way. They reached an old bridge that they would need to cross that linked two sides of a forest. Below the bridge was a small river flowing. The air was crisp and the forest was green. The path was rugged.

"Don't you ever get lonely?" asked Solomon.

"Of course," replied Abraham. "Everyone does at certain times of their lives, but when I work, I feel less lonely. When I travel, I feel less lonely. Nature comforts me. The people I meet comfort me as well. I was married once, but had no children. My wife was the center of my life. She was the reason my heart beat. We met when we were very young children. Her home was near mine. We both came from the same village. I still recall one day when she was ill, I took her for a walk through the village and when she felt too tired to go on, I carried her on my back. Since that day, I knew we would be together forever."

"Why do you refer to her in the past?" asked Solomon.

"Unfortunately, my young friend, she passed away not too long ago," Abraham said. "She became very ill and didn't have the strength to go on."

"I'm very sorry for your loss," Solomon said.

"Thank you, young friend," said Abraham. "I have come to realize and understand that humans were meant to pass through this life alone. Whomever we meet and fall in love with, sooner or later, we lose them or they lose us, but that's how it is. We were destined to walk this journey of life alone, metaphorically speaking or not. Whatever the case may be, we are meant to walk this journey solo and eventually, return back to God."

The two continued to walk through the forest. The mule was lagging behind and needed a break. It was noon. The sun was at its peak straight above. They continued on. The mule was carrying a heavy load that day. Many products needed to be sold. The sounds of pots and utensils shaking and banging against one another kept Solomon alert and focused on the path ahead.

Today's trade route was longer than yesterday's. They spoke little. The sounds around them were loud and distracting enough to keep their minds from wandering off.

"Did you always want to be a traveling merchant?" asked Solomon.

"Like every one, when I was a child I dreamed to be something else," said Abraham. "As a child, I always wanted to be an explorer. I wanted to explore new lands and news places as did the famous explorer, Ibn Battutah."

"Who is he?" asked Solomon.

"Ibn Battutah was an Arab traveler and author," Abraham explained. "He wrote a book called Rihlah which means **Travels**. It was an important source of history and geography for the medieval Muslim world. Battutah was a Berber, which means a person originating from North Africa. He was born in Morocco. He began his first journey in 1325 to Mecca for a pilgrimage. He then covered 120,700 kilometres, extending from Spain in the West to China in the East, from West Africa to the plains of Russia. He had perseverance, wanderlust, and a great curiosity of the world around him. Nothing stood in his way and nothing discouraged him. When he was twenty-one years old, he determined that he would travel throughout the Earth and he did. He spent the rest of his life doing so. At the time of his death, he was renowned as the most traveled person in the world."

Solomon was mesmerized at the story he had just heard. He marveled that a man from one place, with enough determination and will, could travel the world and explore. Nothing was impossible. Ibn Battutah surely faced many critics regarding his travel, but he wasn't affected in the least. Everything was possible. Abraham went on.

"That is what I dreamed to be: an explorer," Abraham said. "As I got older, I found it more difficult to leave and travel far. I had obligations to my family and community. I was compelled to open a shop in my village and become a shopkeeper. Whatever profits I made were for my family. I wasn't the happiest man in the world, but I knew if I was doing something that supported my family, it made me satisfied, albeit not exactly full of joy. One day, while sitting in my shop, a traveling merchant crossed by and sold me products. I asked him where he got his products. He told me that he had gotten them in the city and then he left. When I left, I wondered why I couldn't go to the city myself and purchase products at fair and low prices, and supply my shop. So, I decided to do just that. I closed my shop for a few days and I traveled to the city. Oh, young friend, the city was enchanting! I never imagined in my life that I would see what I saw in the city. The traveling merchant inspired me to go by merely stopping by my shop and selling me a few products. Everything that happens in life is in a sequence of events. I was in my shop that day, then the merchant stopped by and told me a little about the city, and I went to the city myself and became a traveling merchant. I have explored many villages and areas I haven't seen before. I have met many people and understood their minds. I have learned knowledge and different customs from different cultures. God has fulfilled my childhood desire and I earn a living. We will go to the city one day."

Solomon was both excited and nervous to hear that he would too go to the city. He had never traveled outside his village. This was the farthest he'd ever been. He was curious to know what the city was like: the people he would see, the products on display, the noise and attractions. The sun was nearing the horizon on its descent.

"Soon we will go to the city, young friend," said Abraham. "Prepare yourself. You will see life, my young friend."

Solomon couldn't help himself and smiled. He bade Abraham good-bye and began to run in the other direction, where his house was. He was farther today than he had been yesterday, but that wasn't a problem. The farther he went, the more he learned about the area. As he ran, thoughts of what the city was like ran through his mind. The sky was getting darker and Solomon stopped running and walked the rest of the way. He hadn't eaten, but the news of traveling to the city distracted him from his stomach. He couldn't think of anything else except what he would see in the city: the people, the noise, the lights and the attractions. How exciting it would be!

Solomon neared his home. His father was still outside sitting on the terrace in the back. The terrace was square in shape and in the center, a water fountain sprouted out a lovely cascade. Surrounding the terrace were seven trees. Solomon was approaching the terrace where his father was sitting. As he approached, his father looked at Solomon and asked him to sit by him. Solomon sat down without speaking, waiting until his father spoke. They sat quietly looking up at the sky. The stars began to appear and the moon peaked out of the clouds. There was a peace in the air, a peace that nature could always offer.

Solomon's father was drinking a red drink. It was pomegranate juice. He offered Solomon a drink of his juice. Solomon accepted and took his father's glass and slowly drank. The taste was both sweet and sour. The air was cool and the trees stood still. Solomon in that state of peace, couldn't stop himself from imagining what he would encounter in the city. He wanted to tell his father at that moment, but he didn't want to disrupt his father's peace. They both lay in wooden armchairs, staring across the sky, with the fountain in the center sprouting out water.

"Come inside son," Solomon's father insisted.

Solomon walked and entered the house. His mother was sitting in the living room, knitting. She was knitting a scarf for Solomon's sister. Solomon sat down across from his mother, but didn't interrupt her. Every few moments, his mother would look up at Solomon and smile, indicating that she was proud of him. Solomon couldn't bear it anymore. He had to tell her. No one was in the living room, except for Solomon and his mother. His sister was upstairs in her room, probably drawing a picture of horses. His father was in the bathroom, washing up. Solomon decided to interrupt his mother and tell her.

"Mother, please stop for a moment," Solomon insisted. "I want to tell you something."

Solomon's mother stopped knitting and paid close attention to him.

"I am planning to go to the city soon," he said. "The merchant I work for said we had to make a stop there to buy products."

His mother didn't say anything. She continued to knit.

"Did you hear what I said?" he asked.

His mother nodded in affirmation.

"Say something, mother," Solomon appealed.

"Have you told your father?" his mother asked.

"No, not yet," he replied.

"Go and tell your father and then tell me," she said. "He must know. He is your father."

Solomon stood up and walked over to the kitchen. His father was sitting down at the kitchen table, eating bread. Solomon sat down. His father looked at Solomon and knew that Solomon wanted to tell him something.

"Tell me Solomon," his father said. "What's on your mind?"

"Father, today I made my first sale," Solomon said.

"This was the first time I earned my own money. I am meeting new people and understanding their ways of living. I am learning the value of money and how to use it for trade. Soon, I must travel to the city. I will only be gone for two days or so."

His father said nothing. He continued to eat bread

"The city?" asked his father. "Which one?"

"I'm not sure," said Solomon. "It's probably the nearest one to here."

"Oh, that city," said his father. "I haven't been there for ages. It's a nice place. I remember I met your mother in that city. Your mother was the daughter of a fruit vendor, and I would often go to the city to sell my crop. One day, she just happened to be with her father in their fruit stand."

CHAPTER 4 - THE CITY

"When I saw her, I thought she was the most beautiful girl I had ever seen," Solomon's father said. "After that day, I found myself coming to the city more often, just to see her. Some days she wouldn't be there, other days she would. The days that I didn't see her, I would return home saddened and worried that someone else had seen her and had fallen in love with her. Then other days, when I saw her, I did everything I could to show her how much I loved her, without saying a word. I used my eyes. One day, I had gone to the city exclusively to see her. I wore my best pair of black pants and polished my black leather shoes until I could see my reflection in their surface. I borrowed a white shirt from my neighbor and a tie from my father. I wanted to look like a gentleman so your mother would be attracted to me. I shaved, combed my hair back and wore a very strong cologne. I went into the city and the first thing I did was buy a bouquet of red flowers. Most people that saw me walking in the city that day thought I was a politician or minister because the way I walked had impressed many. I had to be confident that day, so your mother wouldn't refuse me. As I neared her father's stand, my heart started pounding so fast and hard that I could hear it in my head. She was sitting in the stand, wearing a yellow flowered dress. Her brown, wavy hair was flowing down across her face. Her brown eyes were big and bright. Her smile was so warm and bright. I couldn't imagine her even speaking to me. I kept telling myself that I had nothing to lose. Whatever happened, I wouldn't be upset or angry. I would have been upset and angry if I hadn't tried to talk to her. I didn't want to lose her or lose the chance of being with her. That was a choice I had to make that day. No pride. I couldn't let self-pride get in the way of the person I wanted. So many people refuse to express their feelings and emotions to someone they love because of self-pride. I call it fear of losing your pride. I knew if she rejected me that day, I would be upset and feel ashamed. Who knows, maybe I would have avoided selling fruit to her father so I wouldn't see her and feel the pain of rejection. That was the risk I had to take and whatever happened afterwards, I was prepared to face it. The least she would think of me was that I was brave enough and bold enough to go up to her and hand her flowers. That is exactly what I did. I just remember walking over. We had seen each other before, so she knew who I was, but this time was different. I wasn't going to sell her father fruit and that was obvious because I came empty-handed, with only flowers in one hand while wearing a suit. I didn't know where her father was at that exact moment, but I felt that heaven above was guiding me and making a way for me to go up to her and talk to her. I did. I went up to her and said, "Hello." She said "hello" back. I then extended my hand and pulled the bouquet over to her and said that they were for her. She smiled and was surprised. She even asked me if they were for her. I said that this bouquet was for the most beautiful girl in the city. Her father then came and was confused as to what was going on. He asked her who the flowers were from and I said that they were from me. He was wondering why and I quickly told him that I admired his daughter and wanted to get to know her, with his permission, of course. He said that it was not his decision, rather it was hers and she had to make the decision. What a shock it was to hear that. At that time, such fathers rarely existed. Fathers were always interfering in their children's lives, especially their daughters'. Most of the fathers of my time were the only decision makers in all of their children's affairs. My father was that way, and I guess that's how I became that way too. It's not completely true, but some parents tend to pass on their behaviors to their children, unless their children decide to change. I was pleased to see a father that would give his daughter the trust and freedom to choose her own path in life. So, at that moment, I looked over to her and smiled and asked her if I could have the honor of taking her out sometime for lunch or dinner. She smiled back and said "yes". I was the happiest man in the world that day. With all the merchants and all the sales that were going on, nothing could compare to the happiness that I was feeling. I had won the heart of an angel, and no gold in the world could compare to her. After that day, we went out a few times for lunch and dinner, and in a few months I went over to her father and asked for her hand in marriage. It was customary to ask the father for his daughter's hand. He agreed and we were married soon after. We lived in the city for a year or two before having children and then decided to move out to a village where I could focus on farming and she could practice her hobby, which was painting. You probably didn't know your mother painted."

Solomon shrugged his shoulder indicating he didn't know.

"She was an artist," said his father. "She would paint pictures of the world, nature, the sky or people. She once painted a portrait of me, holding your older brother, but I don't exactly remember what happened to that portrait. I do recall her painting it."

Solomon was pleasantly surprised. This was the first time he had heard the story of how his parents met. He wondered how many people didn't know how their own parents met or where they met. He was beginning to understand his father and beginning to know the real person within.

"Go son, go to the city and find yourself," said his father. "Meet people as I did. See places as I did and who knows, maybe one day you will find love in the city."

The days went by and Solomon continued to work with the merchant. One day, the merchant decided that it was time to go to the city. That night, Solomon could not think of anything except the journey he was going to take in the morning to the city. He pondered what he would take. A cold air seeped through his window. Solomon walked over the window to seal it shut. As he stood by the window, he reminisced about his life a few years ago. He wondered how so many changes had taken place just recently. Tomorrow he would travel to the city.

The night was dark and the clouds were passing across the sky. Solomon remembered the dreams he had seen and the signs that had lead him to where he was now and to where he was heading. He was now heading to the city. The hours passed and Solomon couldn't sleep. He was too excited to sleep. People couldn't sleep when they were too excited or too anxious.

The sky began to glow. Dawn was breaking. Solomon stood up, stretched his arms and legs and wiped his face with his palms. He took a sack from his brother's belongings and filled it with a few items of clothing. He didn't want to pack too much, as his travel would only last two days or so. Solomon got dressed and walked down the stairs to the kitchen. His father was awake.

"Good morning father," Solomon said.

"Good morning son," his father replied. "Are you ready to go?"

"I am, father," said Solomon. "I packed my bag and I think I'm ready."

"Just remember son, this is a city," said his father. "It's not a village. You will meet many people that have many ways of communicating. Watch your things and money because in the city, you never know who's trying to cheat you. Don't talk too much, rather listen and learn.

Don't fall for the first girl you see, for you will see many. If you need anything, you have an uncle in the city. He's your mother's brother. He has a clothing stall in the city center. Take this card. It has his contact details and address. His name is Sam. He knows who you are, but you were too young to remember him. When in doubt, remember you have family to turn to."

"Thank you father," said Solomon. "I love you." "I love you too son," replied his father.

"Tell mother the same," said Solomon.

"I will son," his father said. "Go before you're late."

Solomon smiled warmly at his father, as his father did the same. Solomon opened the back door and stood on the terrace. The sun was beginning to peak through the horizon. The birds were chirping and bouncing from tree branch to tree branch. Solomon saw Abraham with the mule pass by his house, on the road. He approached Abraham and greeted him.

"Good morning," said Solomon.

"Good morning young friend," replied Abraham. "We must move. We have a long distance to cross. The city is many distances away."

"Where is the city?" asked Solomon.

"There are many cities around," Abraham said.

"The one we're going to is very beautiful and not too far from here. It's called Ladhiqiyah. It's a port city on the Mediterranean Sea."

"Can you tell me anything else about it?" asked Solomon.

"Of course I can," said Abraham. "The city is surrounded by mountains and the sea, so you will find it charming. A lot of business and trading goes on there. If you enjoy smoking, you'll love this city because a lot of tobacco is traded there. It's ancient. It has an old and rich history. It is said to have been founded in the 3rd century BC and ruled by the Phoenicians and Romans. Throughout time, many other civilizations occupied the city, such as the Byzantines, Crusaders, Arabs and Ottoman Turks. The people in the city are friendly and kind to strangers and foreigners. They speak many languages. I guess that's the result of centuries of occupation. One more thing, the girls are very beautiful. I'm sure you will like the city a lot."

Solomon recalled what his father had said to him to not fall for the first girl he saw in the city. He would remember not to.

The path to the city was rugged. The road was long. They often took small breaks along the way. On the road, they frequently met with coffee vendors. The cups of coffee were refreshing and invigorating.

They walked fairly quickly. The sun had reached its highest peak in the sky. Solomon was staring at the ground while he walked and was watching his feet kicking dirt up into the air. He wondered what he would see when he arrived. The distance didn't matter. The pain or fatigue wasn't felt, as long as his mind was kept busy and distracted with thoughts of the city.

Many villages and a few cities were passed. In the villages, everyone knew one another. To Solomon, they were all strangers and he was to them as well. That didn't discourage Solomon from waving hello as he passed by someone on the road or a house with people looking on. People in the villages were often curious of anyone strange to the area. Their lives were so simple and monotonous, that anyone strange to them was exciting.

"They sure stare a lot," Solomon noted.

"It's natural to them," said Abraham. "They mean no harm by it. They are interested in who we are, that's all."

"Should I stare back?" asked Solomon.

"You can," said Abraham. "But not for too long. They want to stare at you, without you staring back. It's awkward if you do. Just briefly look and smile if you want. It always eases the tension and awkwardness."

The day was coming to an end, the sun was slowly setting and they had walked nearly half of the distance to the city.

"We should rest," said Abraham. "We can stop here and rest."

"Where will we rest?" asked Solomon. "On the road?"

"Yes, on the road," said Abraham. "I always do."

Solomon found it strange lying down on the road, but he did anyway. Many trees surrounded the area and the ground was covered with grass. It gave Solomon some cushion as he lay on the ground. Abraham provided a blanket for Solomon to cover himself with. It was very warm and sufficient.

The air was cool and crisp. The sky was a light blue color as the sun descended below the horizon. Solomon took out his sack and noticed a few apples placed inside. His father had probably put them in for him while he was in the kitchen. Solomon offered one to Abraham, but Abraham refused. He pointed out to Solomon that his teeth were unable to chew hard foods, only soft ones. Abraham offered Solomon some water, and Solomon drank some.

That evening was silent and provided solitude. Suddenly a loud noise was heard. Solomon and Abraham were unsure what it was, but it sounded like a wagon. Minutes later, the noise got closer and it turned out to be a horse and wagon. A man was riding in the wagon carrying with him baskets of cotton. As the man approached, he noticed the mule along the side of the road. He stopped by the mule and looked out to see if anyone was there. He yelled out and Abraham answered his call.

"I own the mule," said Abraham. "I'm here, sitting on the ground."

Through the darkness, the man was able to see two human figures sitting on the ground, one being Abraham and the other being Solomon.

"What are you doing on the ground?" asked the man.

"We are merchants," said Abraham. "We are on our way to the city. We have business in the city. We stopped to rest."

"What are your names?" asked the man.

"I'm Abraham and my young friend is Solomon," said Abraham.

"My name is Jacob," replied the man. "I would like to invite you both to spend the night in my home. You can find rest and food, and most importantly, safety. You never know what is lurking in the night and on the road."

"Solomon, what do you think?" asked Abraham.

"I think it's better than sleeping on the side of the road," said Solomon. "It's safer."

"We accept your invitation and thank you for your kindness," said Abraham.

"No need to thank me friend," said Jacob. "This is my service to the Lord and perhaps one day, when I am sleeping on the side of the road, someone will stop for me and invite me to sleep in his home."

Abraham and Solomon stood up and began to follow Jacob. Abraham pulled his mule along. The house was near. Abraham tied the mule to a tree and went into the house, along with Solomon. As they entered, warmth from the wood stove and chimney filled the air. As Jacob walked in, his wife and daughters tidied up the living room.

Jacob had four daughters. All were nearly Solomon's age, and very pretty. Solomon couldn't believe what was happening. Only a few moments ago, he was outside lying on the ground, covered up with an old, but warm, blanket. Now, he was in a warm home, surrounded by four beautiful girls.

"Please, make yourselves at home," said Jacob.

Abraham and Solomon entered the living room, but they first removed their shoes and took off their jackets.

They sat on the floor, which was cushioned by a soft carpet and lined with pillows along the walls. Jacob and his family retreated to the other room in order to give Abraham and Solomon a few minutes to rest before they had dinner. Solomon was mesmerized by Jacob's daughters.

"Oh, his daughters are really beautiful," Solomon said.

"Many girls are in the area," said Abraham. "This is the Mediterranean. Have you not seen many girls in your life?"

"I have, but it has been so long since I've seen one," said Solomon. "The ones that were in my school are all gone now, probably married."

"You have got a lot to see in life Solomon," said Abraham.

Solomon couldn't help wonder where these girls were hiding before and why he hadn't seen girls like them before. He then realized that it wasn't they that were hiding, but he. He was hiding from the world.

"Welcome friends," said Jacob.

"Thank you again for inviting us here," said Abraham.

"We are hospitable people as you know," said Jacob. "This is the Mediterranean."

"Yes we are," said Abraham.

As the two continued to speak, Solomon was anxious to see the girls again.

"I am a traveling merchant," said Abraham. "This is my young friend Solomon. He is joining me and is learning the trade."

"It's very nice to see a young man working hard and learning to trade," said Jacob. "I trade cotton. I also visit the city from time to time and purchase other products. I mostly sell cotton in the area. I have been in this business for years."

"I also trade," said Abraham. "But in various house household products."

"Enough talk of business," said Jacob. "It's time to eat."

The girls reappeared and each carried a tray of food. Plates were passed out, and the trays were placed on the floor. Solomon couldn't control his eyes. He couldn't help himself, and kept looking at each of the girls. Each one of them seemed more beautiful than the other. The oldest one was the tallest and had long black straight hair and black eyes. The second oldest had wavy brown hair and green eyes. The third had shorter black hair and blue eyes and the youngest daughter had wavy brown hair and hazel eyes. It was the youngest daughter that caught Solomon's attention. Her eyes were large and glowing. Her smile was warm and close to the heart. She looked at him, but shyly turned away.

The oldest daughter was outspoken and confident. She entered into conversation between her father and Abraham. Jacob's wife remained quiet and only listened to what was being said. The girls were sitting side by side, in order from oldest to youngest. Solomon sat next to the youngest.

Dinner ended and the girls retreated to their rooms. Jacob's wife sat in the other room. Jacob, Abraham and Solomon were drinking tea. It was customary to have a drink after dinner. They had long conversations about the travels they had had, and the people they had met. Abraham began to yawn and Solomon couldn't stop thinking about Jacob's youngest daughter. He was too embarrassed to ask him what her name was, and it wasn't appropriate.

Jacob left them in the living room, where they were going to spend the night. He closed the door and told them that he would wake them up in the early morning. Solomon wondered if the girl was awake or asleep, and if she was awake, what she was thinking about. Abraham fell asleep and Solomon eventually did too.

Solomon fell into a dream. He saw himself walking along the road in the daytime. Jacob's house could be seen and Solomon approached it. Jacob's daughters were sitting on the terrace. As Solomon approached the girls, he looked for the youngest one, but couldn't find her. The girls appeared alike, staring fixedly at Solomon. As Solomon stared back, the girls simultaneously spoke.

"Read our souls, Solomon." they said.

Solomon awoke to the sound of Jacob and Abraham's voices. The morning had come and Abraham was ready to go. Solomon got his things ready and quietly walked out the door. They both greeted Jacob and thanked him for his kind hospitality.

"My house is open to you always my friends," said Jacob.

"Do you need anything from the city?" asked Abraham.

"Nothing at all," said Jacob. "We will meet again, soon."

As Abraham and Solomon began to walk, Solomon turned his head and stared at Jacob's home. He recalled his dream and what the girls had said to him. Solomon stopped and stared at the windows, hoping the youngest girl would peak out of one. No one appeared. Solomon continued to walk alongside Abraham. He turned back once more, and there she was, peaking out from the corner of the window. Solomon smiled and could only think about coming back to see her again.

Abraham was feeling better, and so was Solomon. The mule was rested as well.

"We will reach the city before sunset," said Abraham.

Solomon couldn't care less about the city, after seeing that girl. She took his mind off work and off his trip. She was a sight for sore eyes.

"Focus with me Solomon," said Abraham. "I know you fell in love back there. I saw your eyes. Remember what I told you, you haven't seen anything yet."

Time went by, and they were closer to the city. Signs were posted showing them in the directions to several cities. Solomon didn't pay close attention to the sign posts. Rather, he only followed Abraham wherever he went.

"Only a few more distances to go," said Abraham.

"How long are we going to stay in the city?" asked Solomon.

"A few days," said Abraham. "When we first arrive, we will rest.

"Is the city were going to the nearest one to my

village?" asked Solomon.

"No, we passed that city a long time ago," said Abraham. "That city is in a completely different direction. The city we're going to is in another direction."

Solomon became worried. His father thought he was going to the nearest city to their village, and not one in a completely different direction.

"My father thinks I'm going to the nearest city to my village," said Solomon. "What if he goes to the city and looks for me?"

"Don't worry," said Abraham. "You're with me. We'll be back soon."

"Where will we rest?" asked Solomon.

"At a place where the sea and sky meet," said Abraham. "Along the seashore."

"I have never seen the sea before," said Solomon.

"I guessed that," said Abraham. "You haven't seen much yet. Welcome to life. Tomorrow, we will begin to shop for bargains. Never buy an item for its stated price. The merchant always increases the cost and expects the customer to bargain. If the customer doesn't, the merchant makes more money and doesn't mind it. If the customer bargains, the merchant has to work harder to earn his profit. Never make it easy for the merchant. Always bargain.

It's the essence of marketing."

They neared the city. The steps seemed to take forever to walk. Many people were passing by on the road. The noise began even before they reached the city entrance.

"We are near, Solomon," said Abraham. "Remember, stay close to me and keep your eyes open."

The city gate was lined with tall palm trees. The sea was visible in the distance as a faint blue mist. Many people were coming into the city. They entered the city and walked up towards the center. Shops were everywhere. People were seen shopping and eating. It was an exciting image for Solomon. Never had he seen so many people in one place and the girls around were breathtaking, as his father had said they would be. The large number of people around overwhelmed him, making him feel as though he was lost in a jungle.

The market was busy. Solomon was carefully following the footsteps of Abraham. As they walked, they passed many shops that were selling clothes, shoes, books, foods and exotic juices. Shopkeepers spoke to all by-passers in many languages, trying to get their attention to attract them to their shops. That's how they competed with one another. The shopkeeper who was louder and more active received more customers.

Solomon was impressed by the activity and energy at the market. It was late afternoon, and the evening was fast approaching. Abraham and Solomon headed for the sea, where they went to set up camp. It was common for travelers to set up camp on the shore of the sea. The rocks provided shelter from the wind, and when necessary, old wooden ships lay on the beach, where they could be used for cover.

As they approached the sea, the smell of salt tainted the air. A warm sea breeze blew on Solomon's face. It was warm and comforting. The seashore was getting near and Abraham and Solomon were getting exhausted from walking. Even the mule was beginning to feel exhaustion. The sea would provide rest.

They arrived and Solomon could only look on in awe. Never in his entire life had he seen such an image, an image that tantalized all of his senses. His sense of sight was overwhelmed by the sight of the wide and seemingly infinite coast and horizon. His sense of hearing was overwhelmed by the sound of roaring waves and crashing tides. His sense of smell was overwhelmed by the scent of the salt from the sea. His sense of taste was overwhelmed by the taste of the sea mist in the air. His sense of touch was overwhelmed by the magical power and energy that the sea breeze carried.

One could only stand and stare at the wonderment and beauty of the sea.

Abraham signaled for Solomon to keep moving. They found a patch of sand that seemed suitable for resting. As they sat down, Solomon continued to stare at the distance and at the horizon. The sea had always been the dream-maker of many. It provided hope, ambition and adventure. It was a constant reminder of infinite possibilities in life and travel.

The shore fizzled as the water retreated back into the sea. The sound brought Solomon a rare comfort. He fell in love with the sea, and it was apparent in his eyes. Solomon could see many men fishing along the coast. Some used lights to attract fish, others stood in the dark.

"Solomon, you see those men?" asked Abraham. "They fish every day. Some catch many fish, and some do not. Some days, luck favors the person who caught none the day before. It's a trade of chance. Though it is, these men never get bored from standing many hours, hoping to catch something. Even if they don't catch anything, they feel blessed that they had the chance to spend the whole day with the sea. The sea speaks to them. It communicates with their inner souls. It removes their worries and fears, and each wave that crashes into the shore washes a bit of pain away, leaving the person at peace. No one leaves the sea anxious. Everyone leaves the sea at peace."

Solomon stared into the horizon as Abraham spoke.

"The sea provides for all, the rich and the poor," said Abraham. "It does not discriminate neither does the sun. The sun will shine on the rich and on the poor and on the educated and on the uneducated equally. The sea follows suit and does the same. The people of this city are coastal people. They are as free-spirited as the sea, and you will learn to see that."

"I can stare out into the sea forever," said Solomon.

"I know you can," said Abraham. "You will have many opportunities to sit and stare out into the sea, and wonder and dream, as many others before you have done. Now, we must try to get some rest. While we are up, would you like something to eat and drink?"

Solomon nodded in agreement. Abraham stood up and walked over to a vendor that sold corn and beans. The vendor brought out two servings and sprinkled a hint of salt on them and squeezed some lemon juice on top of them. This would bring out the flavor of the corn and beans. Abraham and Solomon began to eat. Solomon began to rub his eyes, signaling his exhaustion and readiness to sleep.

"You look tired Solomon," said Abraham.

Solomon nodded.

"Let me tell you a story before you sleep," said Abraham. "Once upon a time, a young boy came to the ocean and found an oyster. He picked it up and opened it. He saw the animal within the shell. He remembered how pearls were produced, by placing one grain of sand into the shell and placing the shell back into the ocean. He made sure the oyster remained in one place, so he placed it inside a cage. He came every day to the ocean and briefly checked on his oyster. He hoped one day to find a large and beautiful pearl awaiting him. The days went by and the boy never became impatient, as he was aware that to wait for something beautiful, one should never rush. So, he never rushed the oyster. Weeks passed and the boy would come to the ocean and check on his oyster and still, no pearl. Months went by, and the boy still came to the ocean and checked on his oyster. To no avail, no pearl was formed. The years passed and the boy grew older. He continued to come to the ocean and check on his oyster and shockingly, no pearl was found. The boy was full of disappointment. Days, weeks, months and years were spent going to the ocean to check on the oyster. In spite of all the effort, no pearl was found. He was saddened and wondered how many years were wasted trying to catch a childish dream that would never become a reality. One day, the boy felt troubled. For years, he had been used to going to the ocean to check on his oyster and finding no pearl. He felt no reason to go to the ocean. On the contrary, the years spent going to the ocean had made him a part of the ocean. The boy decided to go to the ocean again. This time, he was only going to stare out into the ocean. While he was standing, he noticed an old man sitting on the sand. The old man sensed the boy's presence and called him over. He began to speak to him and said how he wished he could only feel the ocean one more time. He told the boy that he was blind. The boy was saddened and asked the old man how he had become blind. The old man told him that he had been a soldier in the war, and an accidental explosion had impaired his vision. The boy felt sympathy for the old man and asked him if he could do anything. The old man asked the boy to carry him into the water, just so he could feel the waves crash onto his body. The boy did as the old man asked, and brought the old man back to his chair. The old man then reached into his pockets, and took out a handful of the most beautiful and sparkling pearls any human had ever seen, and placed them into the boy's hand. He said they were for him and he did not need them, as he could not enjoy their beauty. The boy was shocked and began to cry. He remembered the many years spent in search of one pearl. The moment that he was going to give up, he decided to go on, and finally, the ocean provided. You see, Solomon, never give up. You never know what the ocean is holding for you. Keep hoping and keeping looking forward. It will eventually provide. It provides for all."

Solomon enjoyed the tale and wisdom of the story. Abraham and Solomon laid their heads down as they both faced the sea. Solomon fell asleep and Abraham soon after. Tomorrow would be a new day and a new start for Solomon.

CHAPTER 5 - THE SEA

The morning sun shined brightly on Solomon's face. His eyes slowly began to slip open as the waves of the sea continued to roll over the shore. As his eyes opened fully, he noticed where he was. He was at the sea, the same sea he had stared at for long moments the night before.

Solomon sat up and stretched his arms. His head stretched both ways. Solomon looked around, and to his surprise, saw no one. Abraham wasn't there. The mule wasn't there. Solomon stood on his feet and made a complete turn, but Abraham was gone. He called out to Abraham in a low tone and then gradually increased his volume. His heart began to pound quickly, and he then became anxious. He walked around for a bit, but he couldn't find Abraham. He felt disoriented. The sounds of the waves could no longer be heard. The seagulls hovering in the sky could no longer be seen. Solomon's reality came crashing in, and he began to feel despair.

He wondered how this could happen. He wondered how Abraham could abandon him. He even began to question how he had ended up sleeping on the shore. He began to suspect that, in reality, Abraham had never existed. Many thoughts crossed his mind. He thought of his family, and felt sadness and fear that he might never see them again. Images of his father and mother resonated in his mind. He began to cry. He cried bitterly. The utter loneliness he felt could never be compared to anything.

He sat down on the sand. The sounds of the waves slowly began to be heard as Solomon began to accept the reality that faced him. He began to retrace the steps that were taken the night before. He remembered the market. Solomon put his hands in his pockets and pulled out a few coins. He felt a bit of relief knowing he had some money.

He remembered his father mentioning that he had an uncle in the city, but not in this city. He thought perhaps someone in the city would recognize his name if he mentioned it.

Solomon gathered his belongings and began to walk around. He felt lost. He began to understand why most people never left their hometowns: they feared the feeling of being lost and alone.

The city was beginning to wake. It was early morning and the locals of the city were waking and getting ready for work. Solomon saw a shopkeeper in the street opening up.

"Good morning," Solomon said. "I'm sorry to bother you, but I am wondering if you know my Uncle Sam?"

"I'm sorry, young man, but I don't know anyone by that name," said the shopkeeper. "What village does he come from?

"I don't know," said Solomon. "I've never met him. I only know his name is Sam."

"I am sorry," said the shopkeeper. "I can't help you. I don't know how to find your uncle. There are many people here from many places."

Solomon was in dismay.

"Why are you sad?" asked the shopkeeper.

"I'm lost," said Solomon. "I don't know what to do. I have no one. I'm alone."

"Where are you from?" asked the shopkeeper. "I am from a village," said Solomon.

"Where is it?" asked the shopkeeper.

Solomon began to weep.

"I don't even know where my village is," Solomon sadly told.

"How did you get here?" asked the shopkeeper.

"I came with a traveling merchant," said Solomon. "His name is Abraham."

"Where is this merchant from?" asked the shopkeeper.

Again Solomon wept in disbelief, as he couldn't answer the shopkeeper's question.

"I don't know," said Solomon.

"Young man, how could you leave home with someone you know nothing about?" asked the shopkeeper.

"This is the first time I've traveled," said Solomon. "I really didn't know what to expect. I met the merchant by chance and he offered me a job. He told me that we needed to go to the city to buy products to take back, and I believed him. I was under the impression that the city was the one nearest to my village, but later I discovered I was mistaken. We arrived yesterday, and we slept on the seashore. This morning, I woke up and he was nowhere to be found."

"Do you have any money?" asked the shopkeeper.

"I don't have anything." said Solomon.

"I suggest you walk around the market and ask

around for your uncle," said the shopkeeper. "Who knows, maybe your uncle has a shop in the market. It may even be possible that you find the friend that you came with. Go on, go and look around."

Solomon agreed and left the shop. He roamed the nearly empty streets of the city's markets. The shops were beginning to open. No man with a mule was walking in the city. The men in the streets began to flood the market. Shop after shop began to open. The feeling of loneliness overwhelmed Solomon. The more people that filled the streets, the more lonely he felt. He wondered why he had never felt this way before in the village. The city can be a lonely place when one knows no one.

He asked around for his uncle, but no one knew who he was. There were too many people, and it seemed impossible to find anyone amongst them. Solomon was losing hope. He felt regret for coming to the city. He hated the city and began to feel anger, but the feeling of loneliness was too overwhelming. He couldn't stand the crowds in the street and the noise. He turned back and walked in the direction of the sea. The sea was the only safe place that he felt existed in the city.

He reached the sea and the exact place where he had slept the night before. Solomon looked out into the sea and longed for his family. He felt a peace flow into his heart as a warm breeze comforted his eyes. The Higher Soul was there and knew of Solomon's distress.

"Oh Higher Soul," said Solomon. "I stand in front of this great sea. It seems You are the only One that can understand my sorrow. I am lost in a place I didn't want to be in. I came here with the hope of beginning a new life. I came here with the hope of adventure and exploration. I came here to find something I was missing, to find myself, to find a path to follow, and maybe, just maybe, to find love. Here I sit on the shore, lost and alone. I have no one and no one has me. My family will never see me again and I do not even know how to get back to where I was yesterday. I followed the signs as You showed me. Surely my coming here wasn't in vain. Surely You brought me here for a reason. I feel sadness I cannot deny, but I feel hope that as You brought me here, You will bring me out."

Solomon lay back against the rocks behind him, and stared into the sea. His eyes closed for a moment. As he opened them again, he saw a fisherman setting up his fishing rod across from him. The fisherman was old. Solomon watched him take out his fishing rod and set it up. The fisherman took out a worm from his bucket, and hooked it onto the end of his rod for bait. He stood for hours that

122

day, hardly moving from his place. Solomon looked on, watching the fisherman. He decided to get closer to him, to observe him better. The fisherman noticed Solomon.

"Why do you sit there?" asked the fisherman.

"I was watching you," said Solomon. "What you're doing looks interesting."

"It looks interesting, but it isn't always," said the fisherman. "Some days, you stand here all day without catching one fish. Other days you stand a few hours and catch twenty-five. It all depends on God's blessing that day. Some days are blessed, others aren't. No one knows. I accept this."

"Don't you get tired of standing all day?" asked Solomon.

"I used to when I was younger," said the fisherman. "I was impatient and wanted to catch many fish. The days that I caught fish, I felt strong and proud. The days that I didn't catch fish, made me feel weak. I have come to understand that fishing is not simply to catch fish, but also a virtue that I have learned and it has humbled me. I appreciate the days and whatever comes my way. I have seen many storms and many calm waters. They all have their unique traits."

"When is the best time to fish?" asked Solomon.

"Well in the summer, the best time is during the day," said the fisherman. "In the winter, it is better at night. I prefer to fish whenever I feel like it, no matter the day or time. Man never knows when luck and blessing are coming his way."

"What do you do with the fish you catch?" asked Solomon.

"Some I sell, and some I take home to my family," said the fisherman. "The sea provides. I always keep this proverb in mind. To give a man a fish will feed him for a day, but to teach a man to fish will feed him for a lifetime. This proverb defines life and success."

"Can you teach me how to fish?" asked Solomon. "Do you have a fishing rod?" asked the fisherman. "No, I don't." replied Solomon.

"You can buy one," said the fisherman. "Go to the shop across the street behind you. It's the shop with a big fish logo hanging across the top of it. You can't miss it. Go and buy a rod."

Solomon was ashamed to admit to the fisherman that he didn't have enough money to buy a rod. Nevertheless, he walked across the street and found the shop. He went inside and looked at the rods that hung on the wall. There were many kinds and many different sizes.

Solomon reached into his pocket and picked up the few coins he had. The shop clerk came up to Solomon.

"How can I help you?" asked the clerk.

"I want to buy a rod," said Solomon.

"Have you ever fished before?" asked the clerk.

"No, never," said Solomon. "This will be my first time."

"Let me see," said the clerk. "Since you're a beginner, there is no sense in selling you an expensive rod. Instead, what do you think about this one here? It's nothing special. Its features are basic and good for a beginner."

"How much is it?" asked Solomon.

"Well, what have you got?" asked the clerk.

Solomon showed the clerk the few coins he had. The clerk stood and wondered.

"You don't have much," he said.

Solomon was disappointed.

"Look, here's what I'll do," said the clerk. "I'll give you this one. With the coins you have, you can take it."

Solomon's frown suddenly turned into a smile. It was as if the sun had finally shined on months of rain.

"Yes, I'll take it," said Solomon enthusiastically.

Solomon left the shop with his fishing rod. It didn't matter that it was old, as long as it worked and provided.

He quickly ran back to the fisherman to show him his fishing rod. The fisherman hadn't caught anything yet. Solomon approached him.

"What do you think?" asked Solomon.

"Let me see," said the fisherman. "The line looks old, but I don't expect you to pull out anything heavy. Most fish around here are small anyway. It will do. You have no reel and I don't know how you plan to pull anything out of the water. We'll manage. The pole is thick and strong, so that's good. Well, I see you have yourself a fishing rod."

Solomon smiled with joy. The fisherman began to explain to Solomon all about the fishing rod and how to use it. He tied a hook to the end and attached a worm as bait. Solomon paid close attention. He showed Solomon how to pull out the fish that was tied to his hook. Solomon was learning the basics. The man took a break and pulled out a sandwich which he had stuffed in his coat pocket. He offered Solomon half of the sandwich. Solomon was extremely hungry, and devoured it immediately. The man looked at Solomon and wondered.

"It seems as if you haven't eaten in days," said the fisherman. "What's your story?"

Solomon went on and told the fisherman the whole story, from his village to meeting Abraham the merchant and how he had ended up here, on the sea. While Solomon narrated the story, the fisherman nodded his head several times showing, empathy.

"That's some story," said the fisherman. "I'm sorry to hear that you were abandoned here. I would offer you something, but I don't have much."

"You have done enough," said Solomon. "You taught me how to fish. I thank you."

"You are welcome," said the fisherman. "I tend to come here from time to time. Sometimes, I change my place, hoping my luck will change. I hope we meet again. Stay safe. I must go."

"I will stay here fishing day and night," said Solomon.

The fisherman took his things and left the shore. Solomon stood by, holding on to his rod. Night had fallen, and Solomon remained standing on his feet, holding on to his rod. Solomon remembered the fisherman's words, that no one knew when and where his luck and blessings may turn up. Patience was key and one must never give up.

It was nearing midnight, and Solomon remained where he was. He was about to pull out his hook when suddenly, his rod began to shake. He was startled and held on tight. His rod shook harder and harder, and he held on tighter and tighter. As he held on to the rod, he began to pull his weight backwards. Something heavy was pulling the other way. Solomon was pulling hard and walking backwards when suddenly, a large wobbling fish appeared out of the water. Solomon had made his first catch, on his first day. How blessed he felt! It was just that morning that he had felt alone and desperate, and now, he had learned a skill that would serve him forever.

As Solomon laid the fish down onto the shore, the fish stopped wobbling and Solomon removed the hook from its mouth. He looked at it, and felt like a rich man.

It was dark. Solomon looked around, and saw no one. He didn't want anyone to notice what he'd caught, so he quickly took the fish and retreated. He found an old wooden boat which was turned upside down. It would serve as shelter and storage for his fish. Solomon was feeling less lonely now that he had learned a new skill and caught his first fish. He felt, for the first time, able to take care of himself.

The wind blew lightly that night. Solomon's body was tucked under the old wooden boat. His head stuck out, facing the waves. The sound of the sea was soft and soothing. Solomon's eyes began to shut as he fell asleep.

It was morning and the sun began to pierce

through Solomon's eyelids. He woke to a bright blue sky and warm sea breeze. As he stood up, he brushed the sand off his clothes. He was thirsty and hungry. The fish he had caught the previous night had been laid under the wooden boat, tucked away. He took it out, and walked up the street along the shore. He noticed, fifty meters away, a man setting up a stand. He walked over to the man, curiously wondering what he was up to. He noticed it was a fish stand and that fish merchants usually sold their products in the morning. Small crowds of people began to surround the stand, looking at the different kinds of fish and considering which to buy. Solomon knew he was in a coastal city. People of the coast loved to eat fish, and so, he thought that maybe he could sell his fish and make a profit.

Solomon approached the stand and got the attention of the fish merchant.

"What can I do for you?" asked the fish merchant.

"I want to sell my fish," said Solomon. "Do you want to buy it?"

The fish merchant took a look at the fish Solomon caught.

"It's a good kind of fish and still fresh," said the fish merchant. "How much do you want for it?"

"I don't know," said Solomon. "What are you

129

offering?"

"I'll offer you fifteen coins," said the fish merchant.

Solomon was surprised. Fifteen coins for this fish! He realized fishing was a business. He recalled when he made his first sale to the shop in the village with Abraham, when he only profited one coin. Here, he was selling this fish for fifteen. Solomon wanted to ask for more.

"I'll sell it to you for twenty," said Solomon.

"Sixteen," said the fish merchant.

"By the way, what do you usually sell them for?" said Solomon.

"Only a few coins more than what I offered you," the fish merchant said.

Solomon felt that the man was lying. He could sense something in his eyes that was dishonest. Perhaps the fish merchant would sell the fish for twice the price. Nevertheless, for the time being, it was a good profit. He sold his fish for sixteen coins.

He couldn't wait to get back to the sea and fish again. First, he walked over to a bakery and bought a piece of cake. It only cost him a quarter of a coin.

He was starting to learn the value of the local currency and what it was worth. He finished eating his cake and then went to the next shop and asked for a glass of milk.

That, too, cost him only half a coin.

Solomon headed back to the old wooden boat where he had slept the night before. He kept his money in his pocket. He felt safer, more secure, not alone anymore. He had a new skill that was earning him a living. He took his rod and placed a worm on the end of it. He flung the hook into the sea. He couldn't wait until his next catch. The more fish he caught, the more money he would make.

Solomon stood for hours that day. He noticed a few young boys swimming in the sea. He watched them swim around like fish in a tank. He longed to swim too, but had never learned how to swim. Nevertheless, he placed down his rod and took off his shirt.

The sun was hot, and the water was warm. Solomon tested the water by first placing his foot in it. He slowly walked into the sea. The water covered his entire body and it felt good. It had been a while since Solomon had washed, and being in the water felt refreshing. He didn't go too far, just near the shore where his belongings were. He began to imitate the boys, who were swimming fifty meters away from him. He noticed the way their bodies moved in the water, the motions of their legs and arms, as they paddled their way across the water.

Solomon flopped in the water, uncertain as to

whether or not he was swimming. Later, he came out of the water. His body felt refreshed and the air began to dry the water droplets that remained on his body. He decided that he would swim every morning, as soon as he woke. It would refresh his body and mind.

He sat on the sand and looked out to the sea. His rod lay next to him. Suddenly his rod was pulled out and he was able to grasp the handle. The line was pulled hard, and he pulled back. He managed to pull out the line and noticed a small fish hooked onto it. He was pleased. It was a lot smaller than the fish he had pulled out the night before, but it was better than nothing. That fish symbolized a hard day's labor.

He placed it under the wooden boat. He flung his line into the water again, hoping for another catch. Time went on, and Solomon remained standing and waiting. The sun was beginning to set, but he remained. Though the day wasn't over, he looked forward to swimming again and to selling his catch. No matter what, he would always have something to look forward to the next day, swimming and selling his catch.

The day came to an end and the night began to fall. Solomon sat on the sand, looking out to the sea and wondering if his parents were worried about him. He felt sad that they would never know where he was. He missed them and missed his home, but he could do nothing, expect do with what he had at the moment. Life had led him to a strange city and to the sea. The sea had led him to provision, and he was ready to reap.

The night was never lonely. Nothing could ever be lonely when the sea was near. The sea spoke to people. The sea was a friend to Solomon. It provided him with comfort, trust and loyalty. He lay under the wooden boat, next to his catch. The moon lit the sea and the stars shone above. Memories of his past life in the village came to mind. Those times when he had sat next to his room window, looking up at the stars.

Solomon's eyes began to shut. The waves made a calming sound. He began to dream. He was standing on the shore, the sky grey and cloudy, and the waves strong and rough. A boat was rocking back and forth a few meters out from the shore. A figure stood inside, staring at Solomon. Solomon could not move. The boat got closer and Solomon still could not move. The boat got up to the shore and the figure came out and began to walk up to Solomon. Solomon was afraid, and the figure came face to face with Solomon.

"Look into my eyes, soul reader," said the figure. "Read my soul."

Solomon awoke in a panic. This time, he was not in his bedroom with his mother to call out to. He was alone with only the sea to call out to.

It was dark. The dawn had not cracked yet. Solomon was afraid. He felt an eerie sense of déjà vu. He had seen this dream before, but couldn't recollect the exact time he had had it. The figure had spoken these words to him before. Solomon could not fall asleep again. A sense of fear overcame him. He remained hidden under the wooden boat. As dawn appeared, he felt more at ease. He couldn't wait to swim, but kept having thoughts of his dream.

The sun began to rise, and Solomon stood up. He had plans. First, he would take a swim, and next, sell his catch. Solomon jumped into the sea. The water was a bit cold, but Solomon took his time going in. He went in a bit farther, trying to float. He was swimming a bit better today than he was yesterday. Practice is what he needed. The more he practiced, the better he would get.

He came out of the water and waited to dry. He got dressed and quickly went to the fish merchant. He was there again. He offered Solomon five coins for the small catch. Solomon, comparing the size of the fish he sold yesterday to the one he was going to sell today, felt it was fair. He would have five more coins to add to his account. He felt good.

He went to the bakery, but this time, asked for some bread. It cost him one coin, but this bread would last him the day. Solomon went back to the shore. He sat on top of the wooden boat as he ate his bread. His eyes were fixed on the horizon. After two days of fishing, he had already made a profit. Maybe it was a good thing that Abraham had left him! Otherwise, he would have become a traveling merchant, making small profits. On the other hand, traveling merchants saw the world and met different people, as when Solomon had when he met the daughter of the cotton merchant before arriving in the city. Who knows, maybe fisherman could meet people too!

Solomon took a walk after he ate the bread. He decided to see more of the city. He began his walk in the city's center. Many people were walking around shopping, while others were just observing like Solomon was. The city was new to him, but with each day that passed, it became a little more familiar to him. He noticed the beautiful girls. He also noticed the many shops that he hadn't noticed while coming into the city on the first day.

There were shops that sold animals, perfumes, chocolates and local deserts, musical instruments and other things. He followed a street that led him outside the city's center. The surrounding areas were residential and quiet.

Solomon walked down the street. He noticed a girl sitting on a balcony above the street. She looked down at him suspiciously.

"Are you lost?" asked the girl.

"Do I look lost?" asked Solomon.

"Somehow," said the girl. "I've noticed you walking down the street and looking around as if this was the first time you've ever been here."

"The truth is, this is the first time I've ever been here," confessed Solomon. "I'm curious about the area. I have never seen so many buildings on one street before and so near to one another. It seems all balconies are half a meter away from each other."

"We're near each other and that's what keeps us close to one another. You see all these buildings on this street? Every person living in these apartments knows all the other people and that's a great thing. We still have our privacy, but it is nice to know who the people are where you live and it's even nicer to know that you are also known by the people where you live. You get a sense of belonging."

"You're right," said Solomon. "I grew up in a village. My nearest neighbor was a fifteen-minute walk away. Nobody really knew the other people, only their names. I never grew up the way you did."

"What are you doing here?" asked the girl.

Solomon didn't want to recount the story of how he had been abandoned by Abraham. Instead, he wanted to appear optimistic since good things had begun to happen.

"Well, I'm a merchant and a fisherman," said Solomon.

"Merchant?" asked the girl. "Just like my father."

The girl seemed to be about Solomon's age.

"You're a fisherman too?" asked the girl. "Just like my uncle! You seem a bit young to be a merchant and a fisherman."

"You can't judge a person by his age but by his experience and knowledge," replied Solomon.

"Wisely said," replied the girl.

"What's your name?" asked Solomon.

"Maria. My name's Maria," said the girl.

What's yours?" asked Maria.

"My name's Solomon," he said.

"Where are you staying?" asked Maria.

"I sleep on the shore," he said. "I have to always be alert to the sea and to the fish. No one knows when opportunity knocks, and I cannot risk missing opportunities. The fish come to me, I don't go to them. They decide when they want to come, and I have to be ready to receive them."

"Well, you seem wise for a young man," said Maria. "You're starting to sound like my father."

Solomon smiled and so did Maria.

"I'm a student at the university here," she said. "I study history. Why don't you meet me sometime at the university? I can show you around."

"I would like that very much," said Solomon.

"Maybe you could come down with me to the sea sometime and watch me fish."

"Maybe," she said. "I'm at the university every morning until noon. Just come at noon. You'll see me in the garden."

Solomon bade Maria good-bye and turned back to return to the shore. He felt wonderful. Maria, a local girl, had just made Solomon feel less of a stranger. Girls have that touch. They can always make a boy feel at home. Solomon rushed back to the shore. That night, Solomon could only think of Maria and her nice smile, sweet smell and soft voice. He felt revived.

He lay back on the wooden boat, staring up at the stars above. Suddenly, a shooting star passed across the dark sky, and Solomon whispered to the Higher Soul.

"I am where You guided me to," Solomon said. "I am unsure of the purpose that lies ahead for me. I ask You for guidance and a light to show me the way to the path of my life. Make me the person, You intended to make me."

He fell asleep. He began to dream. He saw himself on the seashore in the night. It felt so real, so vivid. An old woman sat on the opposite end of the old wooden boat. The woman didn't move. Solomon stood up and walked over to the woman.

"Who are you?" asked Solomon.

The old woman didn't reply.

"What are you doing here?" Solomon asked.

Again, the old woman said nothing. He looked at her carefully, and noticed something familiar about her. She wore a long black dress and her hair was covered half way with a black veil. She looked so familiar, but Solomon was unable to recognize her. The woman suddenly looked up at Solomon.

"Solomon, you will be a prince one day," she said. "You have a special power. You will be summoned by many. You will read the souls of the living. This is the message from the Higher One."

Solomon woke frantically. It was dawn. Was it a dream? Was it a nightmare? He could not distinguish. He could hear the waves. He could smell the air. His fishing rod lay next to him. He took off his shirt and jumped into the water. He swam farther than he had ever swum before. He wanted to refresh his mind, refresh his body. He swam hard and long. The water tingled his skin and tongue. The breeze was cool and the waves were subtle.

He felt something move under him. It was a fish. He swam back to the shore quickly, picked up his rod and tossed the hooked line into the water. His body was wet, but began to dry. His eyes were focused and his mind was clear. To catch that fish was the only ambition he had at that moment. He waited. Moments later, the line began to shake. The fish was pulling on the line, and Solomon pulled back harder. He pulled with all his weight and there hung from his rod, a very big fish. He pulled the line closer to him, removed the hook from the fish's mouth and tossed it behind him. He then tossed his rod aside.

He sat down hard and looked straight at the horizon. His mind was not clear again. He felt different. Something was changing inside of him. Something wasn't right. He put on his shirt and picked up the fish. He wanted to sell it, but the merchant hadn't arrived yet.

CHAPTER 6 - THE SOUL READER

The fish merchant was standing by his stand. Solomon approached him. He greeted Solomon.

"How much will you pay me for my catch?" asked Solomon.

"I'll give you twelve coins," said the fish merchant.

"Twelve coins?" asked Solomon. "Look at the size of this fish. It's worth more."

"That's the price I'm offering," said the fish merchant.

"You're taking advantage of me," said Solomon. "You're dishonest and a liar."

"Look into my eyes and tell me if I am lying," said the fish merchant.

Solomon looked straight into his eyes, as they fixed on his own. A warm energy zipped through Solomon's body. His mind could see a dark cave, with a small and faint light glowing in the center. Solomon heard a low and faint voice call out to him.

"Soul reader, I am the soul of this body," it said. "He has neglected me for years. My light was brighter, but has diminished now. I have tried to communicate with him through his mind, but he has not listened. He takes advantage of people and sells them rotten fish. The money he earns, he spends at brothels. He comes home every night intoxicated, abuses his son and bruises him, without reason. Relay this message, soul reader. I have spoken."

Solomon took a deep breath and pulled his eyes away from the merchant's eyes. He turned his head to the side. His head ached. He could not explain what had happened.

"Are you going to sell your fish to me or not?" asked the fish merchant.

The merchant hadn't noticed at all what had happened.

"You didn't hear the voice?" asked Solomon.

"What voice?" asked the merchant.

"Before you spoke to me, how long had I been standing here?" asked Solomon.

"Only a few seconds," replied the merchant.

Solomon felt as if many long hours had passed.

"Take this fish," Solomon said.

"Here are twelve coins," the merchant said.

Solomon looked at the amount and remembered the sixteen the merchant had offered him the first time. He knew that this fish was bigger than that first one. As Solomon turned his back, he said something.

"By the way, I have a message for you," said Solomon. "Stop neglecting your family by spending your money at brothels and on alcohol, stop beating your son without reason, and stop cheating customers by selling them rotten fish."

"Excuse me," said the fish merchant. "Who the hell do you think you are telling me this?" asked merchant.

"I am no one," said Solomon. "I'm only a messenger."

"How do you know my family?" asked the merchant.

"I don't," said Solomon. "I have read."

The merchant stood there confused.

"What magic do you practice, boy?" asked the merchant.

Solomon walked away. He felt exhausted. It was real, no dream. Later that day, Solomon was approached by the fish merchant. Solomon was sitting by the wooden boat, staring at the sea. The merchant cautiously walked towards Solomon. He looked at Solomon for a moment. He wondered whether Solomon was human or super natural.

"Can I ask you a question?" asked the merchant.

Solomon was startled and looked behind him. There stood the merchant, looking afraid and worried. Solomon stood up and faced him.

"Ask," replied Solomon.

"How did you know these details about me?" he asked.

"I don't know," said Solomon. "You told me."

"I never told you a thing about me," said the merchant. "I don't even know who you are. I only know that for the past few days, you have been selling fish to me."

"I don't know what you want from me," said Solomon.

"I need to know how you knew these details about me," said the merchant.

"Why?" asked Solomon. "Are they true?"

The merchant turned and lowered his head in shame, avoiding eye contact.

"I haven't been the best father to my son," he said. "I haven't been the best husband to my wife.

God knows. I know I'm not the most honest merchant in the city. I sold rotten fish to an old lady once by convincing her that it was fresh. I felt bad doing it, but I kept telling myself that it wasn't a big deal and ignored my conscience. I have come home some nights so drunk that I wouldn't recognize my own wife if she stood right in front of me. I have beaten my son many times without reason. My conscience would bother me, but I wouldn't listen. I never thought a day would come when a stranger like you would tell me what you have told me today. Who are you?"

"My name is Solomon," he said.

"Are you human?" asked the merchant. "I am," replied Solomon.

"Can you read eyes?" he asked.

"I do not read eyes or palms," said Solomon. "I read souls."

"You're a soul reader?" asked the merchant. "I thought they only existed in myths and fairy tales. I have heard of myths about some people with the power to communicate with the living soul. I don't know what to say."

"Say nothing," said Solomon. "Instead, heed the warning from your soul."

"I will heed," said the merchant. "I will stay away from alcohol and places that pollute my mind. I will be kind and loving to my family. I will be honest to customers and I will no longer neglect my soul. I will begin to listen. Thank you Solomon."

"Don't thank me, but thank the Higher Soul that guides," replied Solomon.

"I will," replied the merchant.

The fish merchant walked away. Solomon sat back down on the shore. The sea was calm and the sky was blue.

The months passed and Solomon continued to wake early in the morning for a daily swim. His fishing progressed. What he caught, he sold to the fish merchant at an honest price.

Rumors in the city began to spread about Solomon's power. News traveled fast and people gossiped. From time to time, people met with the fish merchant, asking him for details about Solomon's power. They came in groups at times, wondering about the boy with the power to read souls. Regardless of the rumors, Solomon stayed focused on his fishing.

One day, as he stood on the shore holding his rod, a woman walked towards Solomon from behind. Solomon hadn't noticed the woman as his eyes and mind were focused on the sea. She only stared. An hour went by, and she said nothing. Solomon began to feel uneasy.

"Why are you standing there staring at me?" asked Solomon.

"The fish merchant is my brother," she said. "He tells me you have a special power. Is it true? Can you really do what he says you can?"

"I can," replied Solomon.

"Then you know why I'm here," she said.

"No, I don't," replied Solomon.

"You have the power to read souls," she said. "I need to know."

"Need to know what?" asked Solomon.

"I need to know what my soul needs," she said. "Can I come closer to you?"

"Come closer," said Solomon.

"Can you?" she asked.

"You have to invite me to," said Solomon.

"Read my soul," she said.

Solomon's eyes were fixed on hers as he entered a trance. The sounds around him began to fade away. Then, a vision of a blue sky and green field enveloped his mind. A light could be seen. A voice was heard.

"Soul reader," the inner voice spoke. "I am the soul of this body. I live for no one. I have no one to cherish or hold near. I need to love and be loved, but the mind and heart are too afraid of being hurt and broken."

Solomon's eyes were pulled away from the woman's. He fell to the ground and began to breathe hard. The experience once again proved to be exhausting.

"That was fast," she said. "What did you read?"

"I saw a light of goodness inside of you that is surrounded by so much beauty and love, but no one to share it with," Solomon said. "You have always been afraid to love someone for fear of being hurt. The inner light spoke to me. It speaks of a love that it needs. You need to love and be loved."

The woman said nothing. She was shocked at what Solomon had read. For many years, she had avoided falling in love with anyone, fearing heartbreak or pain. She had never had the courage to love or the belief that she was good enough to be loved. The message was clear.

"Thank you Solomon," she said. "Your message gives me courage."

"Don't thank me," Solomon said. "Thank the Higher Soul that guides."

That day, Solomon didn't do much. He just sat on the sand and watched the sea. In the evening, he went for a walk in the city streets. By that time, most people were in their houses or sitting on their balconies. Solomon walked down the street where Maria lived and looked up at her balcony. No one was there. He stood below for a while, waiting to see if she would come out. An hour went by, and then an elderly woman appeared on the balcony.

"Are you looking for someone?" she asked.

"I am," he said. "I am looking for Maria. Is she home?"

"Yes, she is," said the elderly woman. "I will get her. Who should I tell her it is?"

"Tell her it is the boy from the sea," said Solomon.

Moments later, Maria came out on the balcony and looked below at Solomon.

"How long have you been standing there?" she asked.

"Oh, not long," said Solomon.

"How have you been?" asked Maria.

"I've been fine," he said. "Not great, but not bad."

"I expected to see you at the university," she said. "You never showed up."

"I have been occupied with work and business," he said. "That's why I came by tonight. I needed to see you Maria."

They continued on talking for a period of time. They discussed city life, family and friendship. They had a lot of common ideas and feelings about certain things. Solomon was starting to understand the feeling of liking a girl. His heart felt things, and his mind said things, but they both agreed that Maria was someone special.

"Well, I have to get back inside," she said. "I need to study before I sleep."

"I understand," he said. "I just want to say that I enjoyed our talk and I hope you don't mind if I come by here every now and then, to see you."

"I don't mind at all," she said.

Maria went back inside the home. Solomon walked back to the sea. It was night and Solomon needed rest. He didn't want to tell Maria what was really happening with him. The idea that he could read the living souls of people would probably scare her away. That night, Solomon sat on the shore, thinking about where his life was heading. He missed his family. He missed his father, mother, sister and brothers. He imagined that they had begun to believe he was dead, but one day, he would meet them again. He fell asleep while sitting upright.

The morning had come. His eyes opened to waves and calm. He stood up and took off his shirt. He jumped into the sea, and swam hard and far. The cool water replenished his tired body and tired mind. It was too early for anyone to swim. Solomon was the only one in the water. He came out and dried his body. He picked up the rod and stood by, waiting for the right catch. Thoughts entered his mind about the next person that would approach him, wanting to have his/her soul read. Hours went by and Solomon made two small catches. He was pleased. He thought to himself how working made his mind healthy and focused. No matter what happened, he would always work, not for the sake of earning profit, but for the pleasure of the catch itself.

The afternoon came around, and Solomon sat eating a sandwich he had bought earlier. His fish were sold and he had earned a profit. A man walked up to the sea and tossed his hooked line into the water. Every few minutes, he would look back at Solomon. Solomon avoided looking back at the man, even though the man was obviously trying to catch Solomon's attention. The man looked fairly overweight, dirty and untidy. He appeared to be in his forties. Hours went by, and the man remained standing with his rod in his hand. Solomon resumed fishing. He went up to the sea and tossed his hooked line into the water. He stood fifty meters away from the man. The man eventually made his way closer to Solomon. Solomon looked at him and wondered who he was, and what he wanted.

"Don't mind me," said the strange man. "I'm just

fishing here."

"I don't mind," said Solomon. "The sea isn't mine."

"Can I ask you a question?" asked the strange man.

"Sure," replied Solomon.

"Someone has told me about your unusual ability," said the strange man. "The ability to communicate with the supernatural."

"Who told you that?" asked Solomon.

"You know, people talk and people have been talking about you," said the strange man.

"They can talk all they want," replied Solomon.

"Is it true?" asked the strange man. "Are you the boy with the power to see?"

"Why are you asking?" asked Solomon.

"Like anyone, I'm looking for a bit of clarity and direction in my life," said the strange man. "I am looking for a sign or message from above. Can you read my soul? I will give you anything you desire. Just show me a way."

He was obviously wealthy materially. Solomon asked himself how a man, appearing so dirty and untidy, who was so rich in material wealth, could also be so poor in spiritual wealth. If he was content with his material riches, he wouldn't be in search of spiritual guidance. Solomon came to understand, that no matter the amount of material wealth someone acquires, he too needs spiritual direction and guidance to a better way of living.

"You must invite me to read your soul," said Solomon.

"Read my soul," said the man.

Solomon's vision became blurred and overwhelmed. Solomon focused and connected to the man's eyes. He found himself in a place that was strange and sad. Nothing could be seen, but everything could be felt. Solomon could feel the pain inside. A faint light was seen and a voice was heard.

"Soul reader, I am the soul of this body," said the voice. "This body's mind and heart are sorrowful. Greed and envy have rotted the mind and heart of this man. I have suffered much pain and sorrow. This man used to dream of traveling to see new places, but fear of risk prevented him from taking such voyages. His life has become miserable, one that is selfish and angry. He has blamed the world for standing in his way, but all along, it was he who stood in his own way. He lives a life of envy. He envies the people that are living out their hopes and dreams, while he cannot. I have spoken."

Solomon retreated and pulled back.

"Are you alright?" asked the man.

"When you were young, you dreamed of traveling far away," said Solomon. "You dreamed of seeing a barrier that divides a land in the Far East."

The man was absolutely astonished at Solomon's words.

"I have always wanted to see The Great Wall of China," he said.

"Then you must travel and see The Great Wall of China before it is too late," said Solomon.

"I will," said the man. "I don't know what to say. I thank you."

He handed Solomon a small pouch full of gold coins. Solomon took the pouch and nodded his head in gratitude. The man was astonished at what had just happened. He admired Solomon's power and truthfulness.

"You must tell me. What is your name?" asked the man.

"My name is Solomon," he replied.

"Solomon, like King Solomon, the king of ancient Israel?" the man asked. "King Solomon was said to be the wisest king that had ever existed. The Lord gave him the power to control the spirits of the invisible world. He was renowned for being just. You resemble King Solomon. I will call you King Solomon, but you are too young to be a king. I will call you Prince Solomon instead. Thank you Prince."

"Don't thank me, but thank the Higher Soul that guides," said Solomon.

The weeks and months passed. Rumors continued to spread across the city of a boy who could read the souls of humans. One night, he walked up Maria's street. This time, he called out for her. Maria heard her name being called out. She saw Solomon below, looking above, in her direction. Solomon waved to her. She waved back.

"Can I see you?" asked Solomon.

"Yes, you're seeing me now, aren't you?" replied Maria.

"I want to see you closer," he said. "Can you come down and go for a walk with me?"

"I'm not sure," she said. "It's getting late and my family wouldn't feel comfortable with me going out at this time."

"Please, come out for a little while," he said. "I need to talk to you."

"I'll go in and ask my mother," she said. "Wait a minute."

She went back inside, and moments later, she walked out onto the balcony and gestured that she was coming down. Solomon smiled as he saw her walk out of her building.

"I can't stay out too long, and I have to stay on this street," said Maria.

"That's fine," Solomon said. "I just needed to see you."

The two walked up and down the same street several times. They stopped for a moment and spoke.

"People in the city have been talking," Maria said. "They are talking about a boy with a power to read souls. Have you heard anything like this?"

Solomon didn't want to tell her. He wanted to avoid discussing it completely.

"No, I haven't heard anything like this," he said. "Who is this boy?"

"I'm not sure, but rumors have spread around," she said. "People say this boy is cursed or communicates with the supernatural. I think he practices some sort of black magic."

"Well, you know rumors," he said. "Some are made up and some aren't. Who's to know which ones are believable and which ones aren't? I think if someone could read the souls of humans, it would be something good."

"How do you know it's something good?" asked

158

Maria.

"Maria, some people live life without realizing the soul within them," he said. "The soul within constantly communicates with us, telling us how it feels about certain issues and whether or not we should make certain decisions. Also, it guides us to happiness, if we listen to it. Unfortunately, most people live their lives neglecting the soul within and live with no guidance or direction. If this person really existed who has the power to read people's souls, then he could communicate what the soul feels and needs inside, to the person directly, perhaps enlightening his path and giving the person some guidance. I'm sure a lot of people need guidance and direction."

"It sounds scary to know that the soul is communicating with a person about what it feels and needs," she said. "A lot of people too, stop believing that their souls really exist inside them."

"Some people do stop believing, but it doesn't mean the soul doesn't exist," said Solomon.

"I think people should learn to understand their own souls," said Maria.

"Some can, but most can't," he said. "Most people stop listening to what their souls need. They stop believing and stop dreaming. Everyone faces difficulties in life. The darkest hour of the night is the one before sunrise. Unfortunately, most people don't realize that, and give up before the light shines."

"How old are you?" asked Maria.

"How old do I look?" asked Solomon.

"It's not about your appearance," she said. "It's about the way you speak. You talk as an older person, someone who has experienced more than the average person has. In other words, most young guys don't think the way you do. You seem more aware and wiser."

"I hope that's a good thing," said Solomon.

Maria smiled, and so did Solomon.

"By the way, are you still sleeping on the shore?" she asked. "If you are, I wouldn't recommend it. It's not safe. Find a safer place to stay. Good night Solomon."

Maria ran back up to her home. Solomon took his time walking back to the shore. He thought to himself that it would be safer staying at an inn for the night especially since he was carrying a pouch full of gold coins with him. There was an inn across the shore called Seashore Inn. Solomon went to the shore first and took his rod. We went across the street and walked into the inn. It looked rather shabby and old, but that didn't matter. All he wanted was a warm bed and a nice view.

Solomon requested a single bed from the reception desk, and one was available on the sixth floor, the top floor. When he arrived at the sixth floor, the bell-boy led him to his room, room 601. The door to the room opened, and the instant Solomon stepped inside, he noticed the window view of the sea. What a vision! What a sight! All the nights he spent staring at the sea, and all the days spent fishing, still didn't compare to the view he saw of the sea from the sixth floor. It was perfect. The room wasn't five stars, but the view was spectacular. The sea appeared in its true form, with its wide shores, powerful waves that could swallow a city, and the horizon sky, that seemed to stretch forever. A chair was placed at the window, facing the sea. He sat, just staring out to the sea. He felt safe and reminisced about the times he had spent on his windowsill in his room, in his family's home. Now, he was sitting in this room, alone.

He felt a little upset. He missed his family. He missed his home. "No place like home," he thought and even though sometimes the most wonderful place could be facing a person, that was never as wonderful as being home. What could his father be thinking, or his mother be saying? Many questions crossed his mind, but he had to remain focused and optimistic. He knew he would see his family one day, but not this day. He wanted to get some rest, as he was to wake early for his morning swim, and go fishing afterwards. Who knew what people might be in search of him the next day, wanting to hear what their souls were trying to tell them?

Before Solomon retreated to his bed, he looked carefully at the area where he usually slept, down at the shore where the wooden boat was. Two strange men lurked around the area. They seemed intoxicated. One was holding a broken bottle and the other one was holding a thick, wooden stick. They even managed to look under the wooden boat, and when they found nothing, they went on their way. Solomon's heart began to beat faster and sweat covered his forehead. He realized, if Maria hadn't suggested he sleep elsewhere tonight, he could have been seriously hurt, robbed or even worse. This was no coincidence. It was a sign.

Solomon was beginning to feel that he was falling in love with Maria. She cared about him and he cared about her. It seemed so easy being with her, almost too easy.

Solomon decided to stay at the Seashore Inn for a long period. He could swim in the morning, fish in the day and sleep in the room.

He continued to stare at the sea. He had become one with it, as one entity, one body and one soul. In the distance, he saw a fish leap out of the water and splash back in. He recalled the night when he was younger, when his mother explained animal migration to him. She told him how animals migrated seasonally for changes in climate, in search of food or to reproduce. Animals would leave their homes and move from one area to another and then back home again. Birds would migrate in the autumn or spring.

She told him about the Pacific salmon that were born in freshwater streams. They would travel to the waters of the ocean for seven years and then return to the same stream they were born in. When they arrived at the stream, they would lay their eggs and die. They knew that this would happen. They knew a long migration was awaiting them, and that upon their return to the same stream, they would die.

She told him about the green turtle. When it was time to lay their eggs, the female green turtles would swim from Brazil. They would swim to an Island 2,000 kilometers away, an island they had never visited before, except when they hatched from their eggs, as babies. Their swim would be long, and when they arrived, they would plant themselves into the sand on the beaches and dig out holes to put their eggs in. As soon as their eggs were safe inside the hole, they would swim back to Brazil. That always amazed Solomon, how a small turtle would swim that far, and know its way back home. Solomon believed his life was also a migration. He would also return home someday. Everyone finds his way back home, some day.

The morning sun began to come up over the horizon. Solomon had slept on the chair. He woke to the sound of birds chirping. The sun was becoming brighter. Solomon took his rod and headed down to the shore. The hotel receptionist asked Solomon if he was checking out that day. Solomon told him that he was staying another night.

Solomon stepped outside. The warm breeze caressed his face. He went over to the coffee and tea vendor at the side of the hotel. The vendor had a variety of drinks, including coffee, tea, herbal tea, cinnamon tea and an assortment of others. He asked for a cup of herbal tea. It was revitalizing and refreshing. He crossed the street and walked down to the shore.

He went over to the wooden boat, took off his shirt and jumped into the water. It had become a daily routine for him, to have a swim in the morning. How lucky he felt! Many people could only dream of doing this every day.

He swam around, taking dips in the water every once in a while. The sun's light reflected off his tanned skin. When he finished his intense swim, he came out of the water and onto the sand. He picked up a seashell that lay nearby.

The shell was hard. It was so beautiful and bright in many different colors. There were many in different shapes and sizes.

Solomon tossed the shell back into the water where it had come from: back to the sea, back home. He thought it might find its way back home too, just like he would.

Solomon picked up his rod and stood up with his feet planted in the water. He tossed the hooked line in. He hoped for a big catch. The thought of someone wanting to see Solomon for a reading hardly entered his mind. He was too relaxed and too mellow to think about anything else except the sea and fishing.

The afternoon came around. He had caught nothing so far. He wanted a break. He left the shore and walked across the street to a small sandwich stall. He asked for a cheese sandwich, with a cup of tea to drink. As Solomon was eating his sandwich, a strange man walked in and also asked for a sandwich. He sat down at the same table where Solomon was sitting. He looked at Solomon from the corner of his eye, but Solomon's gaze was lowered while he was ate his sandwich.

"Where are you from?" asked the man.

Solomon could barely hear what the man had said, ignored him and kept eating.

"Young man, where are you from?" asked the man in a louder tone.

"Are you talking to me?" asked Solomon. "I am," said the man.

"Why do you want to know?" asked Solomon.

"Excuse me, I was just trying to make conversation," replied the man.

Solomon continued to eat his sandwich, avoiding the strange man's question. The man starred at Solomon while he took bites of his sandwich. It seemed a lot of people were interested in Solomon these days.

"Are you Solomon?" asked the man.

Solomon dropped his cup of tea on the ground and turned in the other direction. He remained quiet and still. The stall vendor cleaned up the mess. The strange man asked the vendor to bring Solomon another cup of tea and sandwich.

"You don't have to do that," said Solomon.

"It's alright," said the man. "I insist you accept my gift."

"I am Solomon," he said.

"I knew you were," said the man.

"How did you know?" asked Solomon.

"Rumors of you have entered every home in the

city. Stories and tales of the boy who can read the souls of people have fascinated the city. You're fascinating Solomon. What is it that happens exactly?"

"Do you believe that every person is born with a power?" asked Solomon.

"Yes, I do," said the man.

"I was given a power to read the living souls of people," said Solomon. "But on one condition."

"What condition is that?" asked the man.

"The person must invite me to read his soul," said Solomon.

"I was sent here to find you," said the man. "Someone very powerful is interested in your service Solomon."

"Who?" asked Solomon.

"I cannot say," the man said. "You must come with me and meet this person, who calls for you."

Solomon's mind began to run. He knew that if he chose not to go, he would forever wonder who this person was that had summoned him, and if he decided to go, he would risk his life and jeopardize his safety. Solomon had faith in the Higher Soul. If anyone was summoning him, he should follow through.

"What's your name?" asked Solomon.

"My name's Adam," replied the man

"I'll go with you," said Solomon.

CHAPTER 7 - THE PRINCESS

Solomon followed Adam to the seaport. A large, luxurious ship was docked on the side. Solomon was convinced Adam wasn't leading him to that ship. To his surprise, Adam did lead Solomon to that ship. Solomon could only wonder who was summoning him. The large ship was rocking back and forth. The crewmen were assembling the items to be loaded on. It seemed Solomon wasn't the only one traveling on the ship. Nearly twenty crewmen were on board the ship. Once again, Solomon's mind was full of wonder and surprise. What person with this sort of wealth would send for him?

Adam led Solomon into the ship. He led him into a lounge that had cushions and carpets on a wooden floor. A bar with stools was in one corner of the room. Next to the lounge was a dance hall. It was a wide room, colorfully decorated, and had a glitzy chandelier hanging from the center of the ceiling.

Adam showed Solomon his room. It was a one-bedroom suite on the second floor with a window view of the sea and a private washroom accessorized with a variety of colognes, creams, shampoos, and soaps. On the wall, a night robe hung next to a pair of black pajamas. Solomon couldn't express his feelings at that moment. Never had he seen such glamour and elegance!

On the roof of the ship was a terrace bordered with a wooden fence. Solomon could not believe this was happening. He was the only guest on this ship. The captain of the ship made an announcement for the crew to board. Adam was already on board and Solomon was above, on the terrace, standing and admiring the view of the sea that seemed to have so many faces. He felt as if it was the first time he had ever seen the sea.

Adam climbed up to the terrace. The ship had begun to move.

"I hope you are enjoying yourself," said Adam.

"I can't imagine myself not enjoying this," Solomon said. "To tell you the truth, this all seems like a dream to me."

"You haven't seen anything yet," said Adam. "Wait until the city is a great distance away from us: you will see the city as you have never seen it before."

Solomon suddenly remembered that he hadn't informed Maria that he was traveling. She would worry if she didn't know where he was. Maria was the only person he had met in the city that actually cared about him. He didn't want to lose that.

"By the way, where are we going?" asked Solomon.

"We are going to an island," said Adam.

"How far away is it?" asked Solomon.

"It's quite far," Adam replied. "We should arrive tomorrow morning. That's a day of sailing, but you'll hardly notice the time. You'll spend most of your time sleeping, eating or sitting on the terrace above."

"Can I fish?" asked Solomon.

"There's no need to fish," said Adam. "We have a large assortment of fish for you to choose from, to have for your lunch or dinner."

"You see, I fish because it brings me joy and pleasure," said Solomon. "It also brought me sustenance at a time where I had none. If it wasn't for the fisherman who taught me how to fish, I don't know where I would be now."

"It's important to always remember where you came from," said Adam. "It humbles a person to realize the hardships he endured. Well, by all means, fish all day if you like."

"By the way," said Solomon. "Who is this person that summoned me?"

A smile appeared on Adam's face as he turned his face away from Solomon.

"I can't tell you," said Adam. "Be patient, you'll meet this person tomorrow."

Adam retreated back to the lower deck of the ship. Solomon stayed on the terrace. He could see in the distance, the wooden boat on the shore that had provided him with shelter on those lonely nights. His eyes began to water as he remembered those nights. Here he was, standing on top of a ship, watching the city become smaller. Wherever he was heading, it was going to change him forever.

It was time for lunch. Solomon walked down to the lounge where tables full of food were placed throughout the room. There were foods he had never heard of. There were meats and salads of all kinds, fruits of every color and flavor. There were desserts made from many different varieties of chocolate. Certainly, this was a meal Solomon would never forget.

After lunch, Solomon went to his room. He lay down on his bed. Solomon closed his eyes, in hopes of passing some time. A few hours later, Solomon awoke and walked into the lounge. There, Adam and some of the crew sat at a table, playing cards and drinking liquor. When Adam noticed Solomon, he immediately stood up and greeted him. He waved for Solomon to sit by him and watch them play. Solomon did. He took a chair and sat next to Adam. The players were aggressive, but having fun. No money was involved. Only pride and honor were at stake.

After the game, Adam and Solomon remained sitting where they were.

"Adam, I was just wondering," said Solomon. "Am I that important to be treated this way?"

"You may see yourself as an ordinary young man in this world," said Adam. "Others may see you the same way, but some may you see your true worth, Solomon. Some people may look at you and see the greatness that lies within. Remember, a beggar may treat you as a beggar, but a king may treat you as a king."

Solomon had heard these words before, but couldn't pinpoint where he had heard them. Nevertheless, they were very wise words.

"You have a power, Solomon, that God has granted you," said Adam. "With this power, you must serve God by serving humanity."

Solomon listened attentively to what Adam was saying.

"Why haven't you asked me to read your soul?" asked Solomon.

"I knew you would ask me that question sooner or later," said Adam. "I guess I am not prepared to listen to what my soul has to say. I am not ready to make the changes I need to make in order to satisfy my soul's needs. You may tell me things that I am not prepared to hear."

"I understand," said Solomon.

"What about you Solomon?" asked Adam. "Who reads your soul?"

"I never thought about that before," said Solomon. "I don't know."

"Where are you parents?" asked Adam.

Solomon turned his head.

"They're home, but I don't know where that is anymore," said Solomon. "Once upon a time, I had a home with my family in a faraway village. As a child, I always felt neglected and uncared for by my father. You see, I had older brothers and they seemed to get all the attention and love from my father. He would often compare me to them, stating how much greater they were than me. That upset me greatly, and many days were spent alone, in my room, staring out of the window at the trees and fields, where I would ponder my life that seemed so lost and unappreciated. When I completed secondary school, my brothers had already traveled away to complete their studies in another country. We never had much contact with one another, and I blamed my father for the longest time for distancing us, in a failed attempt to guide us. I have forgiven myself and my father for what took place in the past. In fact, I miss him the most. Back to the story: one day I took a walk on the road near my home where I had rarely ever traveled. I met a traveling merchant with his mule, sitting by the side of the road. We met and began to speak and he asked me to join him for a walk and I did. I walked with him for a distance and began to learn his trade. He then invited me to assist him with his work and I agreed. The days passed and I learned more and more about trade and commerce. I learned what to buy and how to sell. Soon afterwards, the merchant spoke to me about the city and that he would have to take a trip to it in order to re-stock his merchandise. I told my family that I was going away to the city and my family gave me its blessings. I didn't even know which city I was going to. My father assumed that I was going to the nearest one. I remember passing several, before arriving here."

"What happened next?" asked Adam.

"Well, the merchant and I made our way to the shore, and we assembled our things and rested," said Solomon. "That night, I remember the merchant and his mule, next to me. The next morning, they were gone. There was no trace of either of them. I wonder to myself why I was unable to hear the mule leaving. I'm usually a light sleeper, and the mule makes a lot of noise. Until this day, I doubt ever meeting the merchant, but that doesn't answer the question of how I got here."

"What have you learned?" asked Adam.

Solomon paused and took a moment to think of an answer.

"I have learned how to communicate with other people," said Solomon. "I have learned how to trade and sell. I have learned how to fish. I have learned how to be independent and I have learned how to read the souls of people."

"What you've learned, some people never learn in their entire lives," said Adam. "Some journeys are made without ever noticing the initial footstep. Your journey was a journey of understanding. It's only going to get better and you will see your family again, one day."

"You haven't told me anything about you," said Solomon.

"There is no need," said Adam. "You will have a lot to learn when we arrive tomorrow. It's getting dark. Be sure to get some rest tonight Solomon. Tomorrow morning, we will arrive."

The wind was pleasantly cool that night. Adam retreated to the lower deck. Solomon remained on the terrace, staring at the wide dark sea and the wide starlit sky. Solomon wished that Maria was with him, to enjoy the view that was in front of him. A view like that had to be shared with someone special, or it wouldn't last forever.

He retreated to his room. He put on the pajamas that hung on the wall and got into bed. It was a comfortable bed. His body was accustomed to sleeping on many surfaces and that gave him the ability to distinguish between them and appreciate one more than another.

The morning arrived. Solomon awoke to the sounds of the crewmen shouting outside. As he awoke, he took a look outside and saw something absolutely marvelous. They had arrived at the island. It was surrounded by sand that was as white as snow. Palm trees lined the island shores all around. In the middle, a huge palace stood with a golden gate surrounding it completely. He took notice of the water. It was so transparent that he could count the rocks on the seabed.

Solomon got washed and dressed quickly. He headed up to the terrace. He noticed the crewmen scampering around, trying to figure out where to dock the ship. Adam was busy supervising the crew, but he still had time to greet Solomon.

"Good morning, Solomon," said Adam. "I hope you slept well."

"Good morning, Adam," replied Solomon. "I slept better than a baby sleeping in its mother's arms! Where are we?"

"Welcome to the island," said Adam.

"What island is this?" asked Solomon.

"This island belongs to the Royal Family and that is the Royal Palace," said Adam.

Solomon was unable to respond. Here he was, about to meet the Royal Family. He couldn't believe it. The Royal Family had summoned him, but which member of the family was it that sought his service?

The ship docked and Adam guided Solomon onto the shore of the island. Adam walked up to the gate, as the big golden doors slid open.

"Follow me," said Adam.

Adam led Solomon into the palace. The doors of the palace were large and made of thick wood.

"Solomon, this is where I leave you," said Adam. "You are in the guest sitting quarters of the palace. I was ordered to bring you here. I will leave you now. I must say, you are truly fascinating and well-mannered. May you find your family again, and reunite with your father."

"What shall I do now?" asked Solomon.

"Just wait a while," said Adam. "Your host will be with you shortly."

Adam turned and walked out the door through which he had entered. Solomon was left alone in the sitting quarters. The room was large with high ceilings and marble flooring. Paintings covered the walls, and statues lined the door ways. Solomon was very impressed.

Moments later, a door opened. Solomon's heart raced, and suddenly, everything seemed to move in slow motion as he stared wide-eyed at the door that was opening. Out came a most dazzling sight: a beautiful young woman with golden brown hair, big eyes and a glowing smile.

"Hello Solomon," said the young woman.

Her voice was sweet and innocent. Solomon could not believe it. She knew his name. Never did his name sound as beautiful as it did when she said it.

"I'm Leila," said the young woman.

Solomon tried to greet her back, but was too

overwhelmed. Solomon tried to gather a bit of courage to speak, but found it difficult. Leila was too enchanting to look at. She wore a white dress, and her smell overpowered Solomon.

"You can say something," said Leila.

"Hello," said Solomon, with obvious hesitation.

"You needn't worry, Solomon," said Leila. "Try to relax."

The more she spoke, the weaker Solomon felt. Suddenly, a palace servant entered the room.

"Excuse me, Princess. Would you like anything to drink?" asked the servant.

Solomon's eyes widened.

"What would you like to drink Solomon?" asked Princess Leila.

Solomon didn't respond.

"How about juice?" suggested the princess.

Solomon nodded his head.

"You're a princess?" asked Solomon.

"I am," she said. "Does that bother you?"

"Not at all," said Solomon.

"I hope the journey was comfortable," she said. "It was perfect," said Solomon.

"I'm happy you were able to come here, Solomon,"

said Princess Leila. "I have heard a lot about you."

"Oh, it's my pleasure, really," said Solomon.

"You know, when I heard of you, I felt that I needed to see you," she said. "I needed to understand you and the power that you possess. I have encountered many fortune-tellers that predict the future, but never have I met someone with a power like yours, with a power to read souls. In fact, when I heard about your power, I immediately sent someone to find you. Tell me, did you face any problems getting here?" asked the princess.

"I only experienced the most wonderful hospitality and care," said Solomon.

"I promise you that you will return soon and that you will be paid accordingly," she said.

Even though Solomon had just arrived, as he looked at the princess, he felt a desire to never leave. The drinks arrived and Solomon drank the glass of juice in a single gulp. The sun shone through the room from the windows above, filling it with a warm light.

"Would you like to sit outside?" asked Princess Leila.

"Yes I would," said Solomon. "I would like that very much."

Princess Leila and Solomon walked through the

palace to the other side. A huge garden with cascades and ponds was located in the back. The view of the sea surrounded the palace. They sat in the garden. Solomon felt a peace of mind that was reminiscent of sitting with his father on the terrace at the back of the house, overlooking the field.

Princess Leila's hair blew gently in the warm sea breeze. Solomon sighed at the smell of the princess's hair. It was a moment that Solomon wished would last forever. He and the princess sat in the garden all morning and afternoon, discussing various topics. They enjoyed each other's company.

"Now, tell me something about yourself, Solomon," said the princess. "You left home in search of something. Have you found it?"

"Before I left home, I wasn't alive," he said. "I saw nothing and I did nothing. I asked the Higher Soul to give me guidance to find my way, in order to find myself. When I left home, I was in search of independence. I found it in the city. What I always wanted and looked for was knowledge. When I first arrived in the city, I was in search of sustenance and I found it. The Higher Soul showed me the way. At times of loneliness, I felt His presence by me and I began to truly believe that the sea didn't always offer a fisherman the biggest fish. It may sometimes offer him a small fish. It may have offer him a small oyster, but with a magnificent pearl inside, which is more valuable than any amount of fish. Only the wise can truly understand that."

"Are you satisfied with what the sea has offered you?" asked the princess.

"Well, it led me here," said Solomon.

He smiled at the princess and gazed into her eyes.

"You're handsome, Solomon," said the princess. "Have you found love?"

Solomon blushed.

"Everyone looks for love, no matter what," he said. "From the day we are born to the day we die, we are constantly looking to love someone and be loved by someone. As for me, I haven't had much contact with love in my life, but there is one girl in the city that I met by accident really. I was wandering alone in the city and she spotted me from her balcony. She thought I was looking for something. We talked for a while. I told her about myself and where I came from, and how I arrived in the city. For the first time in my life, someone liked me."

As he mentioned Maria to the princess, he sensed that she seemed bothered. He was certain the princess had become bothered when he mentioned Maria to her. Her eyes told him.

"I'm sure she is a wonderful girl," the princess said. "She's lucky to have met someone like you."

"May I ask you a question?" asked Solomon.

"Yes, you can," said the Princess.

"Do you believe in love at first sight?" asked Solomon.

The princess blushed.

"What do you mean?" asked the princess.

"I mean, is it possible for someone to meet someone they have never met before and feel they have known the person for years? Is it possible to have a feeling from deep within that is unexplainable, at a spiritual level, with feelings of safety, comfort and familiarity? Is it possible to have feelings of joy, pleasantness and satisfaction, from someone a person has just met and to fall in love with that person from that first moment? Do you believe, princess?"

"I have never thought of this question before," she said. "Anything is possible."

"Have you found love?" asked Solomon.

The princess tried to shy away from the question, but Solomon insisted she answer.

"I'm engaged to be married," said the princess.

Suddenly, Solomon felt his heart drop to the ground. His eyes also turned away, lowered to the ground and he was unable to raise them again. He felt crazy for having these feelings towards the princess. He felt he had no right to have them.

"That's wonderful," said Solomon in a tone that obviously expressed unease.

He had just met the princess, had fallen in love with her and was heartbroken all in one day.

"When can I leave?" asked Solomon.

The princess was startled at Solomon's question.

"You want to leave?" asked the princess. "Why?"

"I was just wondering when I could go back to the city," said Solomon.

"I'm sorry if I made you feel uncomfortable," she said. "You can leave whenever you want."

The garden suddenly became quiet. There were no more sounds from the cascades. Solomon and Princess Leila were averting their eyes from one another, but on occasion their eyes would meet.

"Why are you quiet?" asked Princess Leila.

"I see no reason to talk," said Solomon.

"I see," she said. "I'm sorry I asked. Will you excuse me Solomon? I must go inside. I will send a servant to take you to your room. You can leave in the morning. For now, please enjoy your stay and if there is anything you need, don't hesitate to ask."

The princess went back inside, obviously upset and bothered. Solomon was bitter. He wondered how he could have said such a thing to royalty. She didn't even ask him to read her soul.

For the rest of the day, Solomon stayed in his room. There was a balcony with a view of the garden. He didn't know how to undo the damage he had done. He had been sitting with a princess. Now, he would never know where his meeting with her would have taken him. Perhaps they could have become close friends, visiting one another. At least he would have gone through life knowing he was a friend of the princess. That was enough to be proud of. He felt regret that would never go away, for the rest of his life.

Suddenly, footsteps were heard below, in the garden. It was the princess. Solomon panicked. He wanted to go down to see her. Many questions crossed his mind. What if someone saw him walking down? What if she didn't want to speak to him? Worry and anxiety filled his mind. The fear of rejection terrified him. For a while, he stayed on the balcony, staring down at her, as she sat drinking tea. She looked amazing. He didn't want to miss this chance. He had until tomorrow morning to do something and it was already getting late.

Solomon opened his room door slowly, noticing no one in the hallway. He walked across the hall to the staircase and tiptoed down the steps. He passed the kitchen, and made his way to the door leading to the garden. There she was, sitting and staring up at the sky, something he would do. He slowly walked up behind the princess.

"Excuse me, princess," he said. "May I join you?" asked Solomon.

The princess turned and saw Solomon. Her frown suddenly transformed into a smile.

"Of course you can," she said. "Sit by me."

"Nice night," said Solomon.

"Yes, it is," she said.

"I just wanted to say I was sorry for saying what I said earlier," Solomon said. "I was just tired from travel and I needed rest. Please forgive me."

"There is no need to be sorry," she said. "You didn't do anything wrong. I'm usually like that. I am very sensitive and I sometimes overreact."

"Is there anything bothering you?" asked Solomon.

"There is, yes," she said. "You see, I have been suffering. I can't understand why I have been unable to sleep for months, Solomon. I don't know what is wrong with me. I can't sleep at all. I go to bed, close my eyes, and get up from bed even more tired. At times, I sleep in the daytime, but it's never sufficient. Many have heard the story of the king's daughter who could not fall sleep. My father took me all over the world to every expert doctor, but to no avail. I have met with priests, and even witch doctors, but no one was able to cure me. We were desperate, I the more so. Adam, the person who brought you here, said one day that he was in the city and he overheard a fish merchant speaking about you. The man said that there was a boy from an unknown land who can read souls. Adam asked the merchant how he knew of this boy. The man said that you had read his soul and had changed his life. Adam went to see the king, my father, to tell him of what he had learned. My father contacted me and ordered Adam to find you and bring you here, to the island. Ever since my sleep troubles, my father suggested I stay on the island, perhaps for some peace and quiet, but the peace I need is not in my surroundings Solomon, it's inside of me. I need you Solomon. I need you to understand my inner needs, so I can rest again. Can you help me?"

"I would help you with the last breath in me Princess," he said. "Ask me to read your soul."

"Read my soul, Solomon," said the princess.

Solomon fell into a trance, while his eyes were locked on the princess's. A warm feeling overtook him. Soft music was being played in the background. A child's voice was heard, but in a language he didn't understand. A light was seen from up above.

"Soul reader," said the voice. "I am the soul of this body. The holder of me has lost a mother. She has been in great pain ever since her loss. She has had no one to confide in, no one to trust, and no one to love. Her father forces her to marry a man that is not hers. He does not love her, but only loves her name. He does not cherish her, but only her title. She is lost, unable to realize the pain inside and is actually afraid of having this man in her life. Warn her to stay away."

Solomon pulled back his body and closed his eyes. The energy was more intense this time than it had been.

"What did you read Solomon?" asked the princess.

"I have read that you had lost your mother sometime ago and have never really overcome your pain," he said. "You miss her love and security. You now feel alone and insecure. I have also read that your father is forcing you to marry a man you do not love. This man wants to marry you because of what you are, not who you are."

"Oh my God, I can't believe you read that," said the princess, unable to hold back her tears.

Solomon remained silent.

"What should I do?" asked the princess.

"Your soul has spoken to you, Princess Leila," said Solomon. "Do what you feel is right. Listen to your soul. It is always talking to you. You just have to listen and feel."

"Can you promise me something, Solomon?" asked the princess.

"What is it?" asked Solomon.

"Promise me, that whatever happens, you will stay with me," she said. "I believe in signs and miracles, and I believe you were sent to me. I need you."

Solomon's heart felt a warmth and love he had been longing for, the feeling of being needed. She needed him, and he needed her too. How wonderful a feeling it was to belong to someone and someplace!

"I promise you," said Solomon.

The morning had come. Solomon packed his bags for travel. The princess was waiting for Solomon downstairs. Solomon walked down and saw her. He smiled and she did as well.

"When will you come back?" asked the princess with concern.

"Sooner than you realize," he said. "But I have to go and find my family. I have to find them and tell them that I am well and that I have found a home. That home is with you."

The princess was happy, but sad to see him go so soon. She would miss him, but would wait forever for his return.

"Solomon, I have to tell you something," said Princess Leila. "I slept yesterday."

"I was hoping you did," said Solomon.

"Don't be long," she said. "I'll be right here, waiting."

"I promise," said Solomon.

EPILOGUE

Solomon returned to the city. It felt strange again. When he found the place where he belonged, even his childhood memories became strange. There was no time to waste. He told Adam that he going to find his family and that he would look for him upon his return to the city.

Solomon retraced the steps he had taken when he had first entered the city. He found himself on the road, the same road that had led him to the city. Many steps were taken. He felt no fatigue, only the thoughts of the princess that he had fallen in love with.

Days went by with little sleep. Many people were spoken to. Solomon asked many if they knew his father and if so, in which direction his home lay. To keep walking forward was what he often heard. He did, and he kept climbing. Nothing was going to stop him from finding his home and returning to the princess. Many familiar places were passed, and familiar homes. He knew he was heading in the right direction. He could feel it.

The smell of olive trees and orange groves was scenting the air. These scents were familiar. Solomon entered a small shop. The shopkeeper recognized Solomon and asked him why he had stopped coming by. Solomon was shocked that the shopkeeper recognized him. That meant he was near, near to his home.

Solomon began to run, using all the energy left in his body. He ran familiar steps, on a familiar road. In the distance he recognized a field. Solomon's heart began to beat faster. He knew he was near. As he approached the field, it was evening. He had finally arrived home! No one was outside. Solomon approached the front door and knocked. Moments later, the door opened and Solomon's mother stood there.

"Oh my God Solomon, is it really you?" asked his mother.

"It's me mother," said Solomon.

His mother ran out the door in tears and hugged him. Solomon was home again, but he knew where his heart belonged now. It belonged to the princess. He whispered to himself.

"I love you Leila. I'll be back," he said.